Training Her Curves

By

Roxy Wilson

ALL RIGHTS RESERVED

This is a work of fiction. All characters, places, businesses and incidents are from the author's imagination or they are used fictitiously and are definitely fictionalized. Any trademarks or pictures herein are not authorized by the trademark owners and do not in any way mean the work is sponsored by or associated with the trademark owners. Any trademarks or pictures used are specifically in a descriptive capacity. Any resemblance to actual events, locales, or persons living or dead, is coincidental.

Text copyright © July, 2020. Roxy Wilson

Chapter One

Aw shucks. MJ wished she could run and hide, or better yet, that the floor could open and swallow her up. She'd caught sight of him when he was at a distance. It took only a few seconds for her to recognize who it was. Dylan McCoy.

The last time she'd seen him was eight years ago when his sister, MJ's best friend, Leslie, had pleaded with her to come to New York City to help plan his twenty-first birthday party. Leslie had made a compelling case for the trip, pointing out how long it had been since the trio—she, MJ, and Trudy—were able to have some girl time together. It wasn't easy for MJ to convince her husband Rod that she wanted to spend a few days with Leslie to help make the day special for Dylan. Luckily, Rod had suddenly gone on an unscheduled business trip, paving the way for her to help Leslie out and spend a little time visiting with her parents.

The party was an enjoyable event: food, drinks, friends, laughter, and activities galore. But MJ played a lousy game of pool. Although she wasn't an expert at the game, her long hiatus from playing it recreationally shouldn't have affected her game so poorly. Deep down she knew why her concentration was shot: Dylan. He was the reason.

When she'd left New York, he was a darling boy of fourteen, but when she saw him on his twenty-first birthday, after he'd arrived from college for summer break, she was surprised at the transformation. Sure, he was always a good-looking kid, but now he had come into his own. His chest and shoulders were broader, a testimony to his almost maniacal need to keep in shape and eat right. His daiquiri ice-blue eyes seemed more intense than ever before, with just a bit of humor lurking underneath. And he was just altogether...hot. Her new awareness of him made her excited and uncomfortable, hot and embarrassed: a potpourri of emotions, all at once. The way she reacted to the sight of Dylan and his proximity to her that night was...wrong.

Wrong because when she was a thirteen-year-old reading *Sweet Dreams* romance and dreaming about her first kiss, Dylan's mom was reading him nursery rhymes and he was probably dreaming about teddy bears and cotton candy.

Wrong because she was supposed to be happily married, and she wasn't.

Wrong because she should've been thinking about her husband, Rod, but instead she was thinking about her best friend's baby brother. The way he looked, the way he smelled, intoxicated her more than the single glass of wine she'd drunk earlier.

A few times that night she'd wanted to pinch herself for sneaking peeks at him. On one of those occasions he'd caught her staring at him, and she quickly turned away. She was mortified. She tried hard to concentrate on her game, to laugh when it appeared as if someone was telling a joke, and to cheer when someone seemed to have made a brilliant shot. And yet, she barely even knew when it was her turn at the pool table.

"The problem, Marcelle," Dylan breathed into her ear, "is that you've positioned the wrong foot in front."

She didn't even know when he'd snuck up behind her. His body was so close to hers, she became lightheaded. Dylan wielded just the slightest bit of pressure on her hip, prompting her to switch the position of her feet.

"I...I..."

He used his body as a vehicle to steer her a little closer to the table, and then molded her to him and lowered her gently towards the table. "You have to lean into the shots so you can have more control."

I need to control my insane attraction to you, that's what.

MJ barely registered the other things Dylan said to help her to improve her form. Instead, she concentrated on how to breathe her next breath and how to ignore the combination of mint and the remnants of his first alcoholic drink, which teased her nostrils. She called herself all kinds of idiot because she didn't speak one coherent sentence to him during the last few minutes.

The sound of raucous laughter interrupted their little tête-à-tête. MJ was relieved that the other players were distracted by the drunken antics of one of Dylan and Leslie's cousins, who'd had one beer too many.

God. She needed to save face.

And she needed to call it a night.

MJ cleared her throat. "Thanks...for the

lessons, Dylan." She was glad for an excuse to escape his magnetic field.

"Hey, you're leaving already?"

"Sadie and I are heading back to Boston early in the morning." MJ handed him the pool cue.

"Well, the least you could do is to give me my present."

MJ was confused. She'd sent over his present the night before. "Didn't you—"

Dylan pulled her in for a bear hug. A shiver coursed through her body.

He looked down at her, his eyes alight. "I'm glad you came." He pulled in a deep breath, as if he was savoring her scent. But MJ knew better; Dylan wouldn't possibly think about her that way.

Not about such an older woman.

Not about his sister's best friend.

But then he released her, almost as if he didn't want the embrace to end.

"I'm glad I did," she'd managed to say.

After that night, MJ avoided Dylan whenever she went back to New York City for a visit. But since she was home for good now, she'd expected to see him again, just not this soon after relocating to New York City. Sure she knew he was the owner of a fitness center, but she never expected she'd have the bad luck of choosing the one he owned. MJ promised herself to pay more attention to Leslie in the future when she gushed about Dylan's achievements.

She slanted her head to the side so she wasn't facing Dylan directly. Still, she took in everything about him. His black T-shirt didn't conceal the width of his shoulders or his nicely sculptured, tribal-tattooed arms. Dylan's matching black shorts fell a little above his knees, exposing the well-defined muscles on his legs. His champagne blonde hair fell messily over his forehead. In comparison, MJ felt dowdy in her gym rags. She should've taken time to do something stylish with her hair instead of shoving it into a ponytail. Maybe, she should've put some color on her lips. MJ didn't want Dylan to see her looking the hot mess that she was. The last time he'd seen her, she was thirty-four years old and forty pounds lighter. Maybe, he wouldn't recognize her.

"Marcelle?"

No such luck.

MJ turned to face him.

His lips curved into a smile. "You remember me, don't you?"

MJ extended her hand to shake his. "Of course, I remember you, Dylan."

His low chuckle sent tingles up her spine. Dylan ignored her outstretched hand and pulled her in for a hug. Aftershave, a citrus-scented soap, and a scent she couldn't quite define overpowered her senses. MJ groaned inwardly. She shouldn't be reacting to Dylan like this. She'd known him since forever, for crying out loud.

Focus, MJ.

Dylan released her after several moments and MJ could have sworn she saw regret flit across his face, as if he didn't want to let her go. Maybe, she was imagining things. Old age was finally catching up with her.

"It's good to see you, Marcelle. It's been a long time, too long."

As her name rolled off his tongue for the second time, she felt all warm and tingly inside. Dylan reached for the clipboard she was tightly clasping in her hand. It held the data sheet she'd filled out earlier. She'd forgotten about it. His nearness was a distraction. Butterflies fluttered their wings against her stomach. She needed to get her emotions under control. She shouldn't be reacting to a man she'd known since he was a kid.

Come on, MJ. Don't forget the reason why you're here. Get a grip on yourself. There's no time for small talk.

"Uh...Dylan?"

"Mm?"

"Who's going to be my trainer?"

He took his time to answer. "I am. Will that be a problem?"

Yes.

She swallowed and then managed a smile. "No. That's great."

Too late to back out now. She would just have to sweat it. He would probably be too busy to pay attention to her.

He tucked the clipboard under his arm. "Why don't you leave this with me? I'll see you tomorrow at the same time." His lips lifted in a smile. "Can't wait to start on your program?"

"Yeah, sure."

"See you tomorrow, then."

She watched him walk away. Man, but he was hot! It was no wonder her brain froze when he chatted with her. Well, this was an unexpected encounter—she would be more prepared tomorrow.

She would just have to get over this stupid attraction, because nothing was ever going to come out of it. Even if she got past the fact that he was all angles and plains, with that killer body, and she was rolling hills and steep valleys, he was thirteen years younger than she was, for crying out loud. He was practically a kid, and she was an old maid.

MJ exited the building with great speed. On the way home, she picked up a fresh loaf of bread, chicken, and salad. She would make Sadie's favorite spicy herbed chicken tonight. She walked into the apartment, dug into her purse to pay the sitter, and closed the door behind her. After dumping the groceries in the kitchen, she walked into her daughter's room. As always the sight of her daughter's open, friendly face sent a vortex of love slashing through her heart. Her daughter was her pride and joy. To MJ's immense relief, Sadie had adjusted well to the new school and routine. She was thriving, in fact.

As was MJ. With a job as administrative assistant at the law firm of Sullivan and Carter Limited, a new fitness regime, and her own place, everything was under control and life was finally looking good.

And I'm going to rock it.

"Hey, Mom," said Sadie. "How was the gym?"

"It was good. I'm going to start tomorrow." She sat at the edge of Sadie's twin-sized bed. "Are you sure you'll be ok with the sitter while I slog to lose some weight and get in shape?" She knew she was overprotective, but it was hard for MJ to let go of the child who was now a teenager. Nearly a young woman, she reminded herself. "Maybe I should look for an alternative. I could find a gym closer to the office and go in the morning?"

"Mom!" Sadie protested as she made a face. "I'll be fine."

Having run out of excuses to cancel her gym membership, MJ sauntered out of her daughter's room and went into the kitchen to make dinner.

She'd made an effort to locate a gym that wasn't too far from home, one that had the right environment and equipment, not to mention a great reputation. She just hadn't known Dylan owned it. But it would be silly not to join simply because she was going through some serious hormonal imbalance.

Yeah, that's what it was. A hormonal imbalance. Why else would she be attracted to a man who was so much younger?

Oh well! She would just have to rely on her iron will and determination to see her through the gym sessions without drooling over Dylan.

The thing was, she wasn't sure if that was going to work out.

Chapter Two

Dylan groaned inwardly. Working along with Marcelle for the last six weeks was heaven.

And hell.

It was the first time in his career he had to remind himself to treat a client, treat *her*, as professionally as he would any other client.

"Ugh..." Marcelle grunted after she pushed her body back to the starting position to complete her last rep. "Those squats kill me. Every. Single. Time."

Marcelle's chest rose and fell as she fought to catch her breath. "You're a hard task-master."

Not as hard as you think.

Dylan felt himself lengthening within the confines of his track pants. He turned slightly and busied himself with the task of picking up and putting away the equipment Marcelle used during her workout session. He didn't want her to see the effect she had on him.

"I can do it," Marcelle said, pointing to the other equipment on the carpeted floor.

"No worries." He picked up a pair of dumbbells and placed them on the rack. "Off you go."

"Are you sure?"

"Positive. Meet me at the office when you're done."

Marcelle nodded.

Thirty minutes later, she knocked on the door and opened it when Dylan instructed her to come in. Her hair was pinned up at the top of her head in fancy coils and rolls. Her espresso brown skin shone with a radiant luminosity. Her lips were wide and luscious.

A film of perspiration broke out over his skin. The sight of her made his heart race. His body tingled with desire.

Marcelle was skittish around him and had been that way since that undertone of awareness eight years ago. What she didn't know was that he'd inveigled his sister, Leslie, to ask her to help plan his party. He hadn't seen her in years and didn't have a clue how he could get a chance to see her without causing suspicion. His twenty-first birthday party was the perfect opportunity. He'd been unable to hide his feelings for Marcelle, although he wasn't sure if she was able to read the emotion he knew was written all over his face. What she didn't know was that night was the confirmation of what had been brewing inside him for years. He liked Marcelle, but not the platonic way a boy should like his big sister's best friend. At that time she was still married and he had forced himself to back off—but the truth was that his feelings for her were more intense now than they were back then. And she wasn't married anymore.

She was stunning.

She was single.

And best of all, she was genuinely nice and easy to talk to.

Marcelle cleared her throat. "Um...You wanted to speak with me?"

"Yes." Dylan motioned for her to take a seat. "I noticed you didn't seem very pleased at your weigh-in."

She cringed. "I thought after all the hard work I did here, and watching what I ate, I would've seen better results."

Their gazes clashed and then she looked

away.

"You may not have seen much difference in your weight, but your body is changing." Dylan picked up the file, which contained her personal details. "Your measurements show that you've lost a total of seventeen inches in six weeks. That's excellent progress so far." When Dylan saw Marcelle still looked doubtful, he got up from the chair and stood in front of her. He used his finger to raise her chin. "You look great, Marcelle."

Her smile wavered. She stood. "Are you trying to make an old woman feel good about herself, Dylan?"

Old? Her? Where did she come up with that?

"No. I'm trying to tell you the truth; you're perfect." *For me.*

Marcelle considered him for a moment. "If I didn't know better, I'd think you were making a pass at me."

"I'm sure I was." Dylan chuckled. "Thought you would've figured it out by now."

Marcelle's eyes narrowed. "You're kidding me, right?

"Wrong."

Dylan lowered his head. And kissed her. Something he'd wanted to do for years. Her plump lips were as soft as they looked. She tasted of warm honey, cinnamon, and everything sweet and good. He knew he'd caught her by surprise, and he intended to take advantage of the opportunity to deepen the kiss. His tongue licked hers. A low moan escaped his lips. Pulling her closer, he meshed her body with his, feeling the warmth of her curves against his hard muscles. His fingers trailed up her back to cup the nape of her neck. Suddenly, she pulled away. His muscles tensed as he held her for a moment longer. Releasing her, he relaxed and took a careful step back.

He was satisfied to see a befuddled expression on her face.

"Um..." She inhaled deeply and then released her breath slowly. "Dylan...I...We..." She shook her head and moved backwards towards the door. "This should have never..."

"Don't say what I think you're going to say."

She plowed ahead anyway. "The kiss shouldn't have happened. It was wrong."

"From where I stood, it felt right." Dylan took a step towards her. How could she say this? Wasn't this as special for her as it was for him? He'd felt a connection. It was more than attraction. They had something special going on. Ignoring it would be to deny a chance to deepen their relationship in the way he wanted. "In fact, it should've happened weeks ago."

"Come on, Dylan. I'm trying to put the pieces of my life back together again." She pointed at him and then at herself. "I don't want it more complicated than it already is."

Dylan mimicked her gesture of pointing to himself and then at her. "I don't see anything complicated. I like you. And based on how you responded just now, it looks like you like me too."

He dragged his fingers through his hair, frowning at her in puzzlement. Why was she making it so complex? She was tying him in knots, and the worst of it was, he knew she wasn't doing it deliberately. There was not a cruel bone in her body.

Damn it! It feels right.

"I'm trying to get over my divorce..."

"Which happened over two years ago," he interrupted. "And from what Leslie told me, it wasn't your fault. Your ex-husband cheated on you." Her ex-husband was probably a jerk. Only an idiot would let a woman like Marcelle slip through his fingers.

"Since you know about my divorce, you'll understand that I don't want to rush into anything right now, especially with...with..."

"With me?" Dylan took a step forward.

"Yes. It wouldn't be right because...because..."

Dylan cocked an eyebrow. Hell. He wasn't going to make things easy for her. "Because?"

"You're younger than I am," she said.

"And you are more beautiful, so I suppose that makes things equal."

Her mouth hung open for a short, comic moment. "How does that make things equal? What's the age difference between us? Thirteen years."

"Age is just a number. As long as we click...and we do...nothing else matters."

Her lips lifted in a half-smile. "Life isn't as simple as you make it out to be, Dylan. I wish it was, but it isn't."

"It's also not as complicated as you're trying to make it. In my world, when a guy likes a girl, and she likes him back, they go out."

She sighed. "I'm leaving. This conversation never happened...and neither did that...that... kiss."

Yeah, right!

Dylan watched her leave. He wasn't going to let her push him aside so easily. It was fate that brought her back to him, and he was going to make sure she stayed

right where he wanted her to be.
  With him.

Chapter Three

"What the heck was I thinking?" MJ chided herself. "I shouldn't have allowed Dylan to stick his tongue down my throat like that."

But the truth was that the kiss was dynamite. It was better than dynamite. Never in a million years had she thought this man, who was the bane of her best friend's existence when he was a kid, would prove to be such a great kisser.

MJ had been fighting her growing attraction to him. It was difficult to remain unfazed by his close proximity, his touch, when he adjusted her form to ensure she executed her gym routine with precision, or the sound of his laughter whenever she managed to amuse him. She had tried hard to maintain her composure and her sense of decency—but so far it had proven to be a losing battle. She hated to admit it, but there were many naughty things she'd thought about him doing to her and with her.

She wasn't supposed to be feeling this way, darn it. She was supposed to stop the madness. Instead she'd allowed him to kiss her. When he had pulled her closer to deepen the kiss, she had been unable to resist.

His taste, a mixture of mint and the energy drink he'd consumed earlier, made her want the kiss to go on.

Forever!

Come on, MJ. Don't go down that road at all. Not again. Not after what you went through with Rod.

But her mind invariably returned to Dylan and that...kiss, that heartbeat-pumping, hand-moistening, knee-loosening kiss.

MJ forced herself to get her errant thoughts under control, but they kept returning to him.

She had to admit she was pleasantly surprised to discover that Dylan was aware of the circumstances surrounding her divorce. For years she'd blamed herself for her ex's infidelity, and even now, she still found it difficult to face the fact that she was a divorcee. She'd thought her marriage would last forever. Even when Rod cheated on her, she blamed herself for not being able to satisfy him completely. But she hoped that they would have eventually been able to overcome their tumultuous marriage.

The end of the marriage was a blow from which she was still recovering. This wasn't the right time for her to get involved with another man—not to mention with someone who was more than a decade younger. Dylan would simply not do; he wasn't the right man for her. And she'd better keep it in mind. Tomorrow, at the gym, it would be all business. Instructor and client. No more, no less. He would definitely get the message.

Yep. That's how it was going to be.

"Marcelle?" Gina, Mr. Sullivan's assistant, stood opposite her desk, a sheaf of white papers in her hand. "He wants to see you now."

"Who? Mr. Sullivan?" MJ stood. What did he want? Mr. Sullivan was one of the senior partners at the firm. He rarely had anything to do with the administrative assistants who worked in the admin department. MJ was one of the recent additions to the firm. She had very little interaction with the senior partners.

Of course, it could be about the inventory check she'd been conducting for the past month. She'd sent him an email about it yesterday. Yeah, that was probably it.

Gina put her hand on her hip. "Of course, Mr. Sullivan. Certainly, not the pope. And he didn't tell me why he wanted to see you. Do you want me to go back and ask him?" she said with a sneer. With a shake of her caramel colored hair, she sashayed off.

Marcelle bit off the fast retort that came to her lips. She was new to the firm, she was older, and she certainly couldn't afford to make enemies. Most of the people who worked at her level were younger. She was the only late starter in the group. It was hard to befriend this bunch of young, fashion-conscious, career girls who worked all day and partied hard on weekends. In comparison, she was positively boring and staid.

I really need to stop putting myself down. After having come this far, I can make a success of my life.

She adjusted her navy-blue tailored suit, picked up her notebook and pen, and strode towards Mr. Sullivan's office. The senior partners had offices on the upper floor. Unlike the cramped work spaces of the administrative area, the offices were large, plush, and decorated with style. She knocked on Mr. Sullivan's office door.

"Come in." His voice was smooth and deep; much like his personality. MJ had to admit she felt more in common with the senior partners who were closer to her in age than the people in her department. "Hi, Marcelle. How are you?" He gestured for her to take a seat.

A distinguished man; he was tall and lean. His hair, peppery white, added to his mature and conservative look.

"You wanted to see me, sir?"

His smile was easy and unpretentious. "No sir, please. Call me Craig."

"Okay. Um, Craig? Then you can call me MJ. All my friends and family do." *Except Dylan*. He was the only one who called her Marcelle, and she had a profound pleasure in hearing him call her by that name. And in the dead of night, when her thoughts were only on him, she envisioned how he'd say her name when he was in the throes of passion, crying out her name, begging for release.

"MJ?"

Oh my goodness! She had been caught daydreaming. She needed to snap out of it. "Is this regarding the inventory check? I sent you an email yesterday."

For a moment his face was blank. "No. Actually...I called to discuss a more personal matter."

For the life of her, she couldn't figure out what personal matter he wanted to discuss with her. She'd met him only a few times in the past three months. She barely knew the man. "What matter, sir...I mean, Craig?"

He picked up a silver pen from the table and twirled it in his hands. "I was invited to a picnic with some old college friends. It's a sort of a reunion...and I was wondering if you would like to come with me. It's next Saturday."

"Ummm..." MJ had to temper her response to his request, because if she didn't, she'd have to sweep her jaw off the tiled floor. She stared at him.

His lips lifted in a smile. "I know this is kind of unorthodox. It's just that with all the stuff going on lately, I hardly gave the picnic any thought until a few hours ago." He glanced down at his desk and made a sweeping gesture with his hand over the neat stack of files. "I need to unwind and there's no better way to do that, than by doing something fun, with good company. I decided to ask if you'd like to come with me."

Her mind had stopped working. "With you?" God, she sounded like an idiot. Darn it! Couldn't she act mature and confident, like someone her age was supposed to?

"And, of course you know we don't have a policy against socializing with colleagues." Craig stared at her.

Right! He was expecting her to reply.

"Could I think about it? It's just...so..."

Flattering? Gratifying? Unexpected? Yes, yes, yes. She couldn't quite bring herself to say her thoughts out loud.

Dylan's face drifted in front of her.

"...I know, I know." Craig chuckled. "This came out of the blue. Take your time. Let me know in a couple of days." He cleared his throat. It was the first time since their conversation started that he seemed uncomfortable. "And, MJ," he spoke as she stood, the notebook she held forgotten in her hand. "There's no pressure. I don't have any ulterior motives. If you don't want to come with me, there'll be no hard feelings, all right?"

"Of course, yes. Craig. Absolutely." She sounded more and more like a high school kid. Desperate to make her escape, MJ strode towards the door.

"And MJ?" She turned at the sound of his voice. "Good work on the inventory check."

"Right. Thank you, Craig."

As soon as she got out of the room, MJ took a deep breath. Wow! What the heck just happened? Did Craig Sullivan, a senior partner, at the firm just ask her out?

And why the heck didn't I say yes?

Shaking her head at her own stupidity, MJ walked down the corridor. *I'll I call him and say yes tomorrow. Better yet, I'll drop by with the final inventory checklist. His signature is needed for it to be submitted to the CFO. Yes, that's what I will do.*

Once again, Dylan's face materialized in her vision. Darn it! "Go away," she muttered.

"What?" Gina, who was marching towards Craig's office, stopped and glared at her.

"Oh, nothing. I was just talking to myself." Horrified that she'd spoken aloud, MJ strode into the elevator and pushed the button for her floor. It was amusing to see the door close on Gina's haughty face.

Now what? She had an offer for a date with a decent, good-looking, and age-appropriate guy, and here she was, dreaming about someone who just wouldn't do. No, sir. Dylan was definitely not the guy for her.

And she'd better remember it when she

next saw him.

Chapter Four

Dylan counted his client's pull-ups. "Twenty-eight, twenty-nine, thirty. That's it, Tony. Take a break. Drink some water." Dylan wiped the bar with a clean cloth.

Damn! Why couldn't he focus on his work? Marcelle had failed to turn up yesterday. Had she discontinued her training? He didn't think she was the running sort, but maybe he'd managed to scare her off.

Good call, idiot.

Okay. So, perhaps, he shouldn't have put Marcelle on the spot like that. But damn it, he needed to make a move. Needed to push her out of her comfort zone. Needed to let her know he was interested and planned on pursuing her.

He liked keeping her unbalanced...off kilter. He was done with being tactful. Done with waiting for her to notice the subtle hints he'd been throwing in her direction, only to be left feeling hopeless each time she ignored them. He'd attempted to make her see him as more than her best friend's baby brother; now it was time he moved things out of the gym and into...

After finishing the rest of the session with Tony, he checked the clock. Marcelle should be in now. This was her usual time. But what if she had decided to switch gyms?

He went out to the lobby and saw her putting her gym bag in the locker. Breath he hadn't known he was holding released in a sigh of relief.

"Hi."

It was amusing to see the look on her face as she turned to face him. She was gorgeous! The soft yellow workout clothes enhanced her curves and lent a radiant glow to her rich, dark brown skin.

She put the locker key in her pocket. "Hi."

"You didn't come yesterday."

"Sadie wasn't feeling well. She came back from school early."

"Well..." Suddenly, he was at a loss for words. "Let's get to your gym routine."

For the next hour, he monitored her movements, her form, and pace as she worked out.

She's a client. She's a client. Damn it! She's a client.

Dylan mentally reprimanded himself. It wasn't going to work. There was too much heat, too much chemistry between them for him to treat her as just another client.

"Hi, Dylan." Amber, one of his new clients, stopped by to speak to him. At twenty-five, she hardly needed exercise to stay in shape. Tall, willowy, and brunette, she was quite a good-looking girl. Some would say even beautiful, considering the way the other men ogled her whenever she came in. "Could you give me a minute?"

"Sure, Amber. What's up?" He picked up the weights Marcelle had used. After wiping them, he put them back in place.

Amber tossed her long tresses, and leaned towards him. "I was wondering if it would be possible to switch my trainer."

He saw Marcelle walk on the treadmill. *She has a cute butt.* Dylan shook his head. He needed to focus. "Aren't you with Kelsey? Is there a problem?"

Amber fluttered her eyelashes. "Oh, no

problem. Kelsey's good. It's just that I was wondering if you could take me on. I would be willing to adjust my timing according to your schedule."

Dylan frowned, mentally reviewing his allotted time slots. "I'm sorry, Amber. My schedule is full."

"That's too bad." She pouted.

A happy client was a repeat client. "Tell you what, I will drop by on your session tomorrow and see if I can give you a few pointers."

"Sure. That would be great." She sauntered off, her ponytail bouncing with each movement.

He turned his attention back to Marcelle. He caught her staring at him. As soon as he looked at her, she turned away. Amused, he flipped the office keys he was holding in his hand. "Why don't you drop by my office when you're done?"

"Why?"

"Because we have things to discuss." *Private things.* He thought she was about to refuse him, but then a strange expression crossed her face.

"Fine. I'll be there."

Dylan dealt with some of the paperwork as he waited for her. Twenty minutes later, she knocked on his door. He stood and opened it, allowing her to come in.

Shutting the door behind her, he trapped her between the door and himself.

"Why are you giving me the cold shoulder?"

He watched her eyes widen. She crossed and uncrossed her arms.

"Aren't you going to answer me?" Reaching out, he pushed some wayward strands of hair behind her ear. When she leaned away from him, he grinned with amusement.

Marcelle cleared her throat. "I don't think what we did...the kiss...was appropriate."

"Why the hell not?"

"Come on, Dylan. You can't be serious."

She's cute when she frowns.

"I'm more serious than you think."

"I've known you since you were in diapers."

"I can assure you, I don't wear them anymore. Care to take a look?"

Marcelle rolled her eyes. "Oh, please. Let's not go there."

"One of these days you'll go there. And you'll like it." Dylan was delighted when Marcelle's eyes darkened with emotion. Was it desire? He certainly hoped so.

"Listen, kid..."

Is she serious?

"Insulting me will not change the fact that you..."

"No." Marcelle raised her hands as if to fend him off. "Listen, Dylan." She sucked in a breath and then released it slowly. "I'm not sure if you're trying to make a fool of me, or if you're unbelievably..."

"Hot for you?" He finished the sentence.

She lowered her hands. "You're making me uncomfortable, Dylan."

"You're not uncomfortable. Try scared. Why do I scare you, Marcelle?"

Marcelle bit her lips. Dylan waited a few beats but she didn't respond. It was time to up the ante.

Dylan took a step forward. "You want to keep thinking of me like the kid I was before you left, but you know better."

She tried to take a step back but had no room to go as she was already against the door. "You were always too full of yourself."

Dylan chose to ignore her. She was not going to get him off topic.

"When will you come out of hiding, Marcelle? I thought since you were back home, you'd start trying to enjoy life again, but you haven't. I've tried to ask you out and you either choose to ignore me or feign ignorance. So, here's the thing. I'm taking you out tonight, for something light and nutritious, and I'm not going to take no for an answer."

"It's not going to happen."

"Oh, yes, it will. And so will this." His hand moved up her arm.

"Stop it," she said.

"Nothing is going to stop this, Marcelle. You may as well accept it." He lowered his head.

"Accept. This."

Dylan should have known better. But he'd grazed his jaw against hers, and was mesmerized by her fresh fragrance. So taken in by the smell and feel of her, his brain failed to give him a clue about what was going to happen when she pulled her arm back.

She was fast.

And he was too cocky.

Too sure of himself.

There was no time to deflect.

The punch landed in the solar plexus.

Damn.

Chapter Five

MJ sliced carrots for dinner, all the while feeling Trudy's piercing gaze on her.

"So what are you going to do?" Trudy drummed her fingers on the kitchen counter.

"I punched the guy." MJ scraped the carrots into a bowl. "It's like a lawsuit waiting to happen."

Trudy picked up her glass of wine and took a sip. "He's not going to sue you. Not if he likes you."

MJ shook her head as she put the tomatoes in the saucepan that contained simmering stock. She was making stew today. Trudy had dropped by for a quick drink. A friend since high school, Trudy was the first person she called when she relocated to New York City. They made a habit of meeting once a week. Trudy was single, unmarried, and unapologetic about it. She went through guys faster than MJ went through a box of tissues.

Despite the stark contrast in their lifestyle, their friendship had withstood the years they'd been apart when MJ had left Brooklyn.

"Well, the least I can do is call to apologize." MJ stared at the phone, something she'd done several times that day.

It was twenty-four hours since she'd behaved like a fool. Her action brought her no gratification. Instead, her stomach churned whenever she remembered what she'd done. Why did she react so aggressively towards a man, her best friend's brother, a man whom she'd known most of his life and whose only crime was he'd shown more than a casual interest in her?

"Does the fact that you punched him bother you because of your own past history?" Trudy took another sip as she eyed MJ.

Sighing, MJ opened the fridge to take out the chicken she'd already cubed. She put it in the saucepan along with the onions and mushrooms she'd diced earlier. "I suppose it does. Yes."

If she was honest with herself, she would have to admit that her overt aggression was the crux of her current turmoil. It had been an unacceptable act. She didn't condone the use of violence, for any reason. Her behavior had been reprehensible. She'd reacted just like her ex-husband did when he got upset with her. Rod had used his fists on her on countless occasions. He had punched her on her chest, her stomach, and any part of her body that he could grab hold of at the time.

Except for her face. Never her face.

Rod was always careful not to leave evidence of his battering.

MJ had covered her bruises with clothes and hid any signs of pain from her family and friends, with an explanation about some minor mishap at home. She declared herself clumsy or accident-prone, simply because she wanted to protect him. She was always vague when her family inquired, even brushing off questions or concerns with a wave of her hand, so as to ward off any suspicion.

Of course, if he'd hit her in the face, she wouldn't have been able to explain her punch-swollen eyes, or black-and-blue bruises, so Rod left her face unscathed. That didn't mean he never threatened to rearrange it for her if she screwed up one more time. After an *episode*, as MJ used to describe each incidence of Rod's physical abuse, he would warn her that it was the last chance he was giving her, or else...

Her last chance. She'd tried so hard to prevent that time from coming upon her. Her daily life had consisted of walking on a tightrope, trying to avoid doing or saying anything that would raise Rod's ire.

And now she was walking around in his shoes. She'd used the tactics her ex-husband employed—and she hated herself for it.

Trudy finished her drink. "My advice, pal. Call him. Apologize and get it over with. The sooner you do it, the sooner you're off the hook."

MJ nodded. "You're right. I'll call him now."

"I've gotta go. Got a date tonight." Trudy walked over to the stairs and yelled. "Bye, Sadie."

"Bye," Sadie replied.

Trudy shrugged into her coat. With one hand on the door, she turned. "You know, MJ, you need to relax. It really isn't such a big deal that he's younger than you. Most women would love to be in your shoes, to be wooed by a handsome man, to be chased. It's good to be chased. Lighten up. Have fun."

MJ watched her friend stride out and then she put the cubed potatoes into the saucepan. Good advice, but was she willing to take it?

The stew would take some time. In the meantime...

She stared at the phone. She knew she had to make the call in order to make things right with Dylan. But the memories of her past engulfed her, like a forest fire rampaging upon an isolated community.

The life she'd shared with Rod wasn't always miserable, or else she would've been a fool to even consider dating him. Once upon a time, there was laughter, adventure, and romance. Rod had been caring, loving, and attentive.

At a certain point though, things went downhill. While still married she'd been unable to identify the exact cause of Rod's change in behavior. After the divorce, when Marcelle was wrestling with a mishmash of emotions, she'd recognized the exact period in their marriage during which the dynamics of their relationship had changed. It was when their precious little girl, Sadie, showed signs that she wasn't like a typical toddler. Rod hadn't been able to deal with the implications of what life would be like for their family. He was reluctant to join a support group to help them cope with Sadie's special needs and refused to seek the help of a therapist who could've given them the tools they needed to keep their marriage, their relationship, intact.

Then began the quarrels Rod instigated for the most insignificant reasons. Uneasy silences, longer hours at work, and an increasing number of business trips became the norm. These unraveled the thread of the fabric of their unstable relationship. Loud fights, yelling, and the beatings came later.

A private investigator, a box filled with incriminating photos, and a confrontation with Rod, culminated in her receiving several blows to her body—and her face. It was the defining moment of her life. MJ knew that night that it was her last chance to survive infidelity and abuse. So under the cloak of secrecy, she left her marital home, with only Sadie and her dignity as her travelling companions.

The distant beep of a horn roused her from her dark thoughts. Despite what she'd been through, MJ had no excuse for doing what she'd done to Dylan. It was time to get off her butt and make amends.

"Mom." Her daughter came into the living room. Sometimes it was hard to believe that the tall, lanky, beautiful teenager was her child. "Could you please help me with my homework? I've got a science project."

"Coming, darling." She smiled at the light of her life. "I just have to make a phone call first."

MJ watched her daughter leave as she picked up the phone. She couldn't afford to be the person Sadie's dad had been. She was better than him. She would make amends for the wrong she'd done.

And then they would be even, she and Dylan. *Yep! That's it.* She was only doing it to ease her conscience. One phone call and it would all be better.

Chapter Six

If I'd known getting a sucker punch would have landed me a date with her, I would have tried to kiss her a long time ago.

It was that thought which raced through Dylan's head as he sat at the table and looked at Marcelle who was seated opposite him. He couldn't believe his luck when she'd called and asked him to meet her at the health food restaurant for an early dinner. Dylan didn't hesitate to accede to her request and was quick to ask her what time she wanted to meet. As he worked with his clients, he couldn't help but sneak looks at the wall clock, willing its hands to move faster, but time was determined to march slowly. He breathed a sigh of relief when he was done with his last client and bid him a quick farewell.

Now, Dylan watched as Marcelle fiddled with her fingers, avoided making eye contact with him, and looked as if she was searching for the right words to say.

Marcelle cleared her throat. "About the other day..." Her eyes pleaded with him.

"Mmm hmm." The little imp on Dylan's shoulder wanted to make her squirm, even for a short while. It wasn't as if her fist was made of steel. Sure, his stomach hurt a little, but it was his ego that had taken a bruising. He chuckled to himself. He had a feeling this was going to be some fun.

"Umm..." Marcelle hesitated for a second and then she rushed on. "I regret what I did. I've never done that before, and I'm so...so sorry."

Dylan reached across the table and clasped her hands in his. "Answer me this, Marcelle. Do you regret punching me or letting me kiss you?"

Marcelle lowered her gaze, but Dylan waited patiently until she got the nerve to answer him.

"Both."

Dylan felt the wind knocked out of him. He didn't think she'd still have the mistaken notion that they'd done something wrong. They were both single, consenting adults. He thought she would have at least admitted to enjoying the kiss. It wasn't as if he'd stripped her naked and had his way with her against the wall like he'd been so tempted to do. Since Marcelle had come back, he realized she was a temptation he didn't want to resist. Not any longer. And he was done with leaving things to happen at their own pace. He wanted her, probably even loved her, and it was time for him to state his intentions, whether she was ready to hear them or not.

"Marcelle, look at me."

When she didn't, Dylan tucked his finger under her chin and lifted it gently until her eyes made contact with his. "I don't regret a thing." When her eyes widened, he laughed quietly. He knew what she was thinking. "Not even *that*, because it's the reason why I'm here with you today. So yes, I forgive you."

Marcelle took a deep breath in and then released it slowly. She relaxed visibly. Dylan caressed her chin with his finger and then released it quickly, lest his luck ran out.

Marcelle chortled as if she read his mind. The sound of her laughter was like sweet music to his ears.

"So, now that I'm back in your good graces again, let's order our dinner and enjoy the rest of the evening," he said.

"Sounds like a plan."

Wow. It looked like he was right after all. The day was shaping up to be a good one.

If only Marcelle would ease up about their budding relationship. But yeah, in time he had every intention of making her see that he was the right choice for her. They had everything going for them; in fact, he couldn't remember the last time he was so at ease with another woman.

The waiter took their orders. After he left, Dylan leaned forward, his eyes focused on her as she sipped her drink. "Do you remember that birthday party...it was that kid's, James."

She put the glass down. "Oh yeah, the neighborhood bully. His hair was as orange as carrots."

"He was tormenting me, trying to make me get into the dark room where his father's gardening tools were stored. Since he was about a foot taller, there wasn't much I could do as he pushed me into the door. And I tried to resist. And you sort of swooped in, grabbed hold of his collar, and pulled him back."

"I put the fear of God in him." Marcelle's

pearly teeth flashed as she recalled the memory.

"You were my hero," he said.

The waiter chose that moment to bring their food. When he left, Marcelle picked up the fork and picked her salad apart. She set it down again.

"And that incident should remind you that I am thirteen years older than you. How can you even think of...us as having some sort of relationship?" She dabbed the napkin on her lips. Dylan suspected it was a ruse to win her some time to think about a suitable response to stop him in his tracks. "Sure, we can be friends. I've got no problem with that, but..."

I wasn't off base at all.

He sighed. Why was she so hung up on their age difference? They had so much in common; who cared if she was older? "Love has nothing to do with age or race or class..."

"Love?" She sputtered.

He immediately regretted saying that. Now she would back off even more. "Forget I said that." He raised his palm up. "And tell me something honestly; if age wasn't a factor, would you date me?"

"Yes, sure. You're a good-looking guy, ambitious, easy to talk to. But you can't deny our age difference."

"And I don't want to deny it. I just want you to put it aside for a little while. Just erase it from your mind, make it vanish. And then judge me as you would any other guy."

She took a bite and swallowed with care, almost as if she was giving herself time to think about what he'd said. "I can't." She shook her head. "I think...I would never be able to get past it."

"I see it's a major hurdle in our romance." He took a bite of his sandwich.

She moved her hand back and forth, first pointing to him and then to herself. "We're not having a romance."

"Oh yes we are. And we've already had our first fight, and survived it. Major brownie points for us. Yeah!"

A chuckle escaped her lips. "You're so persistent."

"You betcha!" He enjoyed seeing her laugh. She hardly did that, almost as if she dared not allow herself to enjoy even such small, carefree moments.

In an attempt to stay on safer ground, Dylan took Marcelle on a trip down memory lane. They both laughed as they remembered childhood friends and incidents. The conversation flowed easily.

Finally, the waiter came to take their orders for dessert. "I couldn't eat another bite."

"Sure, you can! Their grilled apples with cheese and honey are divine."

"I really shouldn't…"

He put his hand on hers. "It's fairly nutritious, and besides, I'll make you burn it off in the gym," he promised. He could think of other ways he could help her burn off the calories she'd consumed, and none of them had anything to do with working out at the gym. They placed their orders. Dylan looked down at their intertwined fingers; it felt right.

She broke the moment when she pulled her hand away. "How's Leslie?"

"Good as gold. Climbing the corporate ladder as planned."

"She was always hardworking and ambitious. I miss her since she moved to Chicago."

"Brooklyn is in her blood. She won't be able to stay away for long," he said with confidence. "Just like you couldn't."

She looked away.

"Sorry. It just slipped out." He put his hands on the table, hating that forlorn look on her face.

Stupid! Why did he have to say that?

"It's all right. It wasn't meant to be, and I do like being back home." She ran her finger over the edge of the table.

The waiter brought their dessert. They both dug in.

"This really is delicious." She licked the spoon, her tongue darting in and out.

His heart missed a beat. *Talk about delicious.* He could probably gulp her down in one big bite. But he didn't want to scare her off when they were doing so well. *Take it slow, take it slow!* He reminded himself. "The chef is a client. He's extremely innovative. Coffee?"

"No. I really should be getting back. The sitter is going to leave soon and I don't want Sadie to be on her own in the apartment. I mean, she's fifteen, but I hate leaving her alone for long."

"Cool." He signaled the waiter for the check. "Oh, no you don't." He put his hand over hers as she dug into her purse for her wallet. "It's my treat."

"But why? I called you."

"I asked you out first." He gave cash to the waiter.

"But..."

"Hey! I am an old fashioned guy. My girl doesn't pay her own way on a date." He strolled over to her chair and adjusted it, making it easier for her to stand.

"I'm not your girl, and this wasn't a date."

He laughed as he opened the restaurant

door, gesturing for her to step outside. "You keep denying that right till the end if that makes you happy."

They walked to the parking lot where he'd parked his SUV. As they neared the car, Dylan took out his key and pressed the button. The car beeped once. "Shit!" He ran over and bent to take a look. "Damn!"

"What happened?"

"Someone slashed the tires." He circled the vehicle.

"All of them?"

"Damn it!" Dylan ran a hand over his face. "Okay. No worries. We'll take a cab, and I'll call my mechanic to take it to the shop."

"But shouldn't we call the police or something?"

"Hey! This is Brooklyn. You think the police are going to pay any attention to a petty act of vandalism?" He held her arm as they crossed the street. "Come on! I'll get you home."

"I'm just worried about your vehicle."

"It's not a big deal. Probably some kids wanted to blow off some steam." He shrugged his shoulders. "The same thing happened to me once before."

He hailed a cab and helped her in. It had been such a fun date that he didn't want to allow a minor setback to mess with his mood.

Whether Marcelle admitted it or not, they'd just had their first date—and he had many more in mind.

Chapter Seven

She shouldn't have been having such a good time, but she was woman enough to admit that Dylan was lots of fun to be with. MJ had forgotten what it was like to enjoy the company of a man, a man who was thoughtful, had a great sense of humor, and was attractive.

MJ shook her head. Why was she thinking of Dylan when she was supposed to be working? Admonishing herself, she tried to concentrate on the three-page memo she was drafting. Her fingers flew over the keyboard as she finished the job and hit print. The printer hummed gently and spewed out the papers. After scanning the document to make sure she hadn't left any typos or spelling mistakes, she clipped the pages together and dropped them into the outgoing pile. It would be delivered later to the Head of Administration.

To her great surprise, she had discovered that she actually enjoyed her job. The fact that she was managing to keep up with the younger crowd was a matter of pride for her. Initially she'd had to work really hard at brushing up on her typing skills; and it took her a while to learn how to deal with office politics, but now she was in her element. She performed her duties with clock-like precision, finishing jobs that were assigned to her, submitting them on time, and efficiently delivering proposals.

She checked her email: nothing new. It was nearly five. Time to go home. Her eyes drifted towards the phone for the umpteenth time as she considered calling Dylan to ask about his car. *No. No. No.* Doing so would only encourage him. And what would be the point of that? She had no intention of dating him.

Did she?

No, she didn't. Damn it! Why couldn't her traitorous heart agree with her mind? Dylan wasn't the right choice. No, not at all. It wasn't that there was anything wrong with him—but for goodness' sake, she couldn't just ignore their age difference as easily as he wanted to.

Perhaps, it was because he was the first man who had tried to woo her with such consistency since her divorce. MJ wasn't vain, just realistic enough to admit that it wasn't hard for her to attract attention from men. But she'd been deliberately keeping the shutters down, forcing anyone who gave her any hint of attention to back off.

Maybe she needed to focus on someone else. It would take her mind off Dylan.

Yep! That's what she needed to do.

"MJ?"

"Yes, Craig!" In an unconscious gesture, she smoothed down her skirt as she stood. What was he doing here?

A sheepish grin crossed his face. "I know I told you to take your time, but I was wondering if you'd made up your mind."

What was he talking about? With a jolt she realized. "Right! The picnic!"

How could she have forgotten? This had to be fate. One moment, she thought about dating another man, and the next moment, Craig was standing in front of her. *Thank you, God!*

"So what did you decide?"

Dylan wasn't the right choice, but Craig certainly was. It would be stupid of her to say no. "Yes, I'll go with you."

A look of profound relief darted across his eyes. "I am glad. Is it okay for me to pick you up at about eleven in the morning?"

"That's fine."

"Great. Now, all I need is your address."

Feeling slightly numb, she gave him her address. "I'll see you."

"Looking forward to it. Dress casual. It's just a bunch of old college buddies."

When he left, she flopped down on her chair. Going out with Craig was the right decision.

But then why did her heart feel as if she had betrayed someone about whom she cared deeply? Dylan's face flashed across her mind, and she closed her eyes, willing herself to forget him.

No. It wouldn't do to dwell on what could never be.

At 5:30, she left the office and headed for the gym. After her workout, she showered, and zoomed straight for the door. Dylan blocked the way.

"Hey, where's the fire?" He laughed. A clipboard was shoved under his arm, and a white band kept his messy hair off his forehead. He oozed with unbridled sex appeal. The man should be banned from showing up in public looking like that.

She couldn't face him just now. She

simply couldn't. "I just need to get home."

He grabbed her hand as she made a beeline for the exit. "Slow down, tiger. I've got something for you."

"What?" She adjusted the strap of her shoulder bag. Her eyes caught a movement and she looked up to see Amber sashay by. If looks could kill, she would have dropped down dead that very instant. Amber's gaze focused on their clasped hands, her eyes darted to Dylan and back to MJ.

"Come with me." Without letting go of her hand, he led her towards his office.

"What's up with Amber? Is she angry at me?"

He opened the door and ushered her inside. "Why do you say that?"

"Just...that look she gave me."

"Oh! I am afraid that was directed at me. I..."

"What?"

He turned to face her, boxing her in between the door and his hard, muscled body. She could smell the spicy cologne he favored. "Never mind her."

"I want to know."

"Fine. She asked me out yesterday, and I turned her down."

An unfamiliar emotion reared its ugly head in the depths of her heart.

Jealousy?

Certainly not. She had no reason to feel such a thing. It's not like she had a claim on Dylan. "She asked you out?"

He trailed a finger down her cheek. "I told her I was…otherwise occupied."

MJ chewed her bottom lip. "Dylan!"

He put his finger on her lip and tugged it free. "I didn't mention it, because I didn't want to make you upset."

"I'm not upset."

"I've been hooked on you for a long time, Marcelle." He leaned forward and his lips left a trail of kisses down her cheek and into the side of her jaw.

The scent of him drove her mad. Before she could succumb to his presence, MJ blurted, "I'm going on a date on Saturday."

"What?" He straightened. What was that unfamiliar emotion in his eyes? Anger? She had never seen such an icy look in his eyes before. "What did you just say?"

"Someone asked me out, and I said yes."

"Are you crazy? What about what's happening between us?"

Remorse, and something akin to regret, coursed through her heart. "That's what I've been trying to tell you." She put a finger on his chest. "There is no *us*. And there never will be."

He ran a hand over his face. "You're lying. I don't know why you're determined to deny your true feelings, but fine. If this is something you want, then go for it. I hope it helps you get through whatever mental crisis you seem to be having. But let me assure you, you'll want to come back to me. If not now, then later."

"I'm sorry, Dylan. It was never my intention to hurt you."

"But you're doing exactly that. You're ripping my heart out, and the worst part is that you don't even realize you are doing it." He took a step back. "Go."

She slunk out of the office. Her heart felt as if it would break into two. That terrible look in his eyes told her that she'd lost his trust. The knowledge of what she'd done shredded her confidence that she'd done the right thing.

Would he ever forgive her? And would she ever be able to forgive herself?

Chapter Eight

MJ braced herself as she entered the picnic area, her arm on Craig's. It was a little intimidating to meet his friends, although if she had to admit it, for a first date, a casual picnic was best. She'd taken care to dress in a smart, milky-white blouse and a pair of umber Bermuda shorts. Her diet and exercise regimen was beginning to pay off: she looked and felt better about her appearance, and she was proud of how good she looked today.

MJ relished the scent of freshly cut grass, mixed in with meat grilling on the barbecue. And the sight of bare-back boys kicking ball helped to calm her frayed nerves and reminded her that summer was her favorite season.

"Hello, Craig!" A woman, dressed in a tank top and cargo pants, came to greet him. "It's been a while." Two men joined them.

Craig made the introductions. MJ made the appropriate noises, shook hands, smiled, and was glad when she was dragged off by a friendly, plump woman towards the picnic table.

"Thank you."

"Sorry about that! We're a noisy, overwhelming bunch. I'm Karin. And you are?"

"Marcelle. Craig's date."

"Ah!" Karin dug into an ice box and handed her a bottle of cold light beer. "That explains it."

MJ picked up the bottle opener and popped the lid. She took a swig. "Explains what?"

"The way the women swarmed around you. The men, of course, did the same because they're…you know…men." Karin laughed.

MJ blinked. "Thanks for the compliment. But why did the women swarm around me, as you so succinctly put it?"

"Craig's been divorced for seven years, and this is the first time he's brought someone to the picnic."

MJ's throat tightened, and she took another big swig from the bottle. "That does explain it. She waved a hand to fan her face. "Is it just me or did the temperature rise another degree?"

Karin chortled. She opened a beer. "Don't worry. I'm sure you can take the pressure. Come on, I'll give you the lowdown on everyone." She began to walk around the picnic area which had been laid out with care. Several long, low tables were set up, replete with ice boxes, bowls filled with potato salad, and trays of sandwiches and chips. Someone was grilling meat patties in one corner. MJ followed, noticing the quiet, casual way people sat on low benches or on blankets spread on the grass.

"You guys do this every year?"

"Yep! We meet once a year. There are thirty-seven of us in New York City. Some people come over from other cities and states. It's fun, easy to manage, and it's nice to catch up with old pals. Some bring dates or spouses and others, like me, come alone."

"There you are. I thought I'd lost you," Craig said. He was holding a beer in one hand and the other was gripped by a woman who was dressed within an inch of her life. Bold, bright red lipstick graced lips; mascara and eyeliner enhanced her baby blue eyes; and her hair, a slick sheet of brownish-orange, spun down her back. "Karin, it's wonderful to see you." Craig freed his hand to give a hug to MJ's guide. "Thanks for taking care of my date."

"Always at your service." Karin raised her bottle. "Angela, what a pleasure to see you. It's been a while."

"Ah, yes, I believe introductions are in order." Craig beamed happily, oblivious to the cold frost emanating from his friend. "MJ, this is Angela, an old friend of mine. Angela, MJ."

"Pleasure," she shook MJ's hand limply. "There's someone I haven't seen in a long time. I must say hello to her." With a quick toss of her hair, she took off.

What was that about? MJ shared a glance with Karin.

"Come, let's take a walk." Craig placed his hand in the small of MJ's back and then faced Karin. "Would you care to join us?"

Karin laughed. "Sorry, I'll only be the third wheel, getting in your way. Bring MJ to the table later. Bill's patties—if he doesn't manage to burn them like last time—are usually divine."

As they wandered off, MJ fought to find a subject to talk about. "Perfect weather for a picnic, isn't it?" Damn it! Couldn't she have picked a better topic?

"Sure is." He smiled. "I hope you're not feeling awkward in this crowd."

"No. They all seem nice. Loud, noisy, and fun."

"We could go somewhere else if you're not comfortable."

"No. I'm fine, really!" Better to be in the company of fifty other people than to be alone. What did people talk about on first dates? Her dinner with Dylan had been so easy, spontaneous. *Shut up! Shut up!* She silenced that one-track thought in her head. *Don't you dare think about Dylan!*

Craig cleared his throat. "So you're originally from New York City?"

"Oh yes. I grew up in Brooklyn. After marriage I moved to Boston, but then...after my divorce I came back here with my daughter."

"How old is she?"

"Fifteen."

"I have twin boys." Pride licked his words. "They're thirteen. Their mother and I share custody."

"Divorce is a bitch." It slipped out before she could censor the words. "Sorry."

He laughed. "I'm a divorce attorney, MJ. I hear much worse than that a hundred times a day. Some of my clients..." He shook his head.

"Do you like it? Being a lawyer, I mean."

"Never wanted to be anything else. I love it. The never-ending paperwork, the marathon to the courts, and the clauses in the contracts. It's my life."

"It's important to enjoy your work, isn't it? Not that it should become the center of your world, but it's essential to take pleasure in it." Her eyes focused on three boys who were playing ball. A solid kick landed the ball next to Craig's feet. He kicked it, returning it to the boys.

MJ and Craig turned back. "Do you like your work? I suppose I shouldn't really ask you that…"

"No, it's fine. I love it. When I started, I was a bit nervous. After being at home for many years, I wasn't sure if I would be able to get back into the routine, the pressure of deadlines, and office work. But, there's joy in it. A quiet kind of joy."

He nodded. "That's a nice way to put it." Craig turned, as a portly man approached them. "Ah! Warren. It's good to see you, man! It's been two years."

The man huffed and puffed as he drew closer to them. He enveloped Craig in a hug. "Made it in time. Just came back from Spain three days ago."

"Warren, this is MJ."

"Nice to meet you." Warren's gaze wandered to her, and then back to Craig. "I tell you, Craig, that's a country. The opportunities in Europe are huge for a serious investor."

MJ followed the men as they got involved in a long discussion about corporate mergers, long-term bonds, and interest rates. She spied Karin at a table and joined her. Time flew as she chatted with Karin, who had a daughter the same age as Sadie. They exchanged information about schools, craft programs, and the triumphs and tribulations of being the mother of a teenage girl. Someone handed her a paper plate with a hamburger on it. She ate potato salad and made a quiet vow to put in an extra half-hour on the treadmill. When it was time to leave, she found herself exchanging a warm hug and her telephone number with Karin.

"Call me," Karin said.

MJ walked with Craig to the parking lot.

"Would you like to go for coffee?" He asked after they sat in the car.

"No, thank you. Sadie's at a friend's house, but she is going to be back at four, and I just don't like leaving her for long." MJ smiled. "Sorry about that."

"No problem." He popped in a CD and switched on the air conditioner. "Hope you weren't bored. Warren just took over, and we hadn't seen each other in a long time."

MJ was honest enough to admit that she'd had a good time with Karin. "It was fun. I liked your friends, especially Karin."

"She is a gem of a person. Warm and kind. Generous to a fault," he agreed.

Thirty minutes later, he drove the car into the parking lot of MJ's building.

Suddenly feeling conscious, she freed the seat belt. "Umm..."

"Thank you for a lovely day," Craig said.

"I had a good time."

They both stared at each other. Craig tapped his fingers on the steering wheel. "I think I pretty much ditched you. That Warren..."

MJ shook her head. "It's okay. I had a great time. Really!" Craig leaned in, just a little bit. He wanted to kiss her. Unnerved, she scooted back, and opened the car door. "I really should go."

"Wait!" He gripped her hand. "I don't believe in wasting time, MJ. And I sense the vibrations here. You're not going to see me again, are you?"

A breath expelled from her lips. *God! Did he have to be so direct?* "You're a great guy, Craig."

"Ah! I hear a 'but' coming."

"It's not you...it's..."

"There is someone else, isn't there?"

To say that she was shocked by his perception would have been an understatement. "No. Yes...I mean..." MJ closed the car door as embarrassment flooded through her. "I'm sorry. I never should have come with you."

"Don't be silly. So what if we can't be...I mean, can we be friends?"

"Yes, of course." She grabbed the lifeline he offered. He really was a sweet, courteous man. A gentleman. Too bad her heart was elsewhere.

"Thank you for being so wonderful, Craig." She touched his cheek. "Thank you."

"I'll see you in the office."

She got out of the car and waved as he left. Trust her to make a mess of this. There was nothing wrong with Craig. By all standards, he was perfect for her—but what could she do with her traitorous heart that was stuck on Dylan?

Darn it! There was no mercy for fools.

And she had been nothing but one.

Chapter Nine

Dylan performed another set of push-ups, stood, stretched, drank a bottle of water, and dove into another set. Finally, he stood and wiped his brow. He reached for the weights.

"Are you trying to kill yourself?" He glanced at Kelsey who'd come in quietly while he was busy working out.

Dylan sat, lifted the weights. His muscles ached in protest as he pushed himself to the limit. "I know what I'm doing. Is there something you want?"

She came in and closed the door behind her. Nearly ten at night, the gym was deserted. "Something's up. I can tell."

Kelsey had been working at the gym

since he started, and she knew him far too well. It would be hard to shake her. "Just something I'm working out of my system."

She sat on a press bench. "Should I warrant a guess?"

"No."

She plowed on. "It's MJ, isn't it? I thought something was brewing between you two, but she's been avoiding you for a couple of days. And today you practically ran when you saw her coming in, so my guess is that this sudden onset of superhuman activity has something to do with her."

"Go away."

"Ah! My theory has just been confirmed."

Dylan ground his teeth. Kelsey was nothing if not tenacious. And she was a good friend who didn't deserve to be brushed off. "She doesn't like me...that way."

"Why? Is there something wrong with her eyes or her mind?"

Her loyalty touched his heart. "Apparently, she has decided that she's too old for me."

Kelsey sputtered. She opened her mouth, closed it again. "Ahem!"

"What? Nothing? No wise remarks or pearls of wisdom to share with me?" He stopped to take a breath and decided he'd punished himself enough for today.

"I can see why she'd think like that?"

"Please! Don't tell me you agree with her?"

"I never said I agreed with her. Just that I can understand why she would be hesitant to...start a relationship with a younger man. People would talk."

"People talk all the time. One can't be scared of the judgment of others and refuse to live life to the fullest. She's..." Frustrated, he ran a hand through his sweat-drenched hair. "Whatever. It's over anyway. She's seeing someone else."

Kelsey stood. "Are you sure about that?"

Dylan picked up his towel and slung it around his neck. "Why?"

"It's just that she called ten minutes ago. She was looking for you."

"Why the hell didn't you tell me?"

"I'm telling you now. When I told her that you were exercising, she hung up. Didn't leave a message."

Why would Marcelle call him at this time? Hadn't she made it abundantly clear that she didn't want anything to do with him? "It's late." He looked at the clock. "What did she want?"

"She didn't say."

"I'm going to take a shower and swing by her house on my way home."

Kelsey raised an arm. "Go, Dylan!"

"Oh! Get lost." He practically ran into the shower. Maybe something was up? What if something had happened to her daughter? Maybe she needed help? Dread twisted and coiled through his mind, leaving him feeling anxious.

"Allan, close the gym, will you?" He tossed the keys to his manager who was loitering in the reception area. Since he was always the last one out, he was sure his manager was suitably shocked as he stared at Dylan's retreating back.

He drove to Marcelle's house, straining himself to stay within the speed limit. As he parked the SUV and strode towards the door of the lobby, Dylan began to question himself. She'd snubbed him. Worse, she'd ditched him for another man. And he came running like a puppy when she called. What if she called to tell him she wouldn't be coming to the gym anymore? He would look like an idiot if he showed up at her doorstep and all she had to say was goodbye.

His hand stilled an inch away from the buzzer.

An elderly man opened the building's door with his key. "Are you having trouble, young man?"

Knowing he had little choice, he walked

inside behind the man. "No. I came to visit a friend."

Striding up to the elevator, he pressed the button to her floor. He'd read the nameplate on the main entrance and knew she was in 5B. After a moment's hesitation, he pressed the bell of her apartment. A young girl, the mirror image of Marcelle, opened the door.

"Yes?"

"You must be Sadie?" He smiled, amused to see how much she looked like her mom; the same bearing, same espresso brown skin, and locks, the color of ripened blackberries.

"Who are you?"

"Could you tell your mom that Dylan's here?"

"Dylan?" Marcelle came out into the corridor. "Come in, please." She ushered him inside and then turned to her daughter. "Sadie, baby! Why don't you go to bed and sleep."

Dylan's heart jackhammered against his chest. Even dressed in a well-worn pair of jeans and a sleeveless, cotton candy-pink blouse, Marcelle looked resplendent. Her skin glowed with a healthy luster.

"Okay." The girl lumbered off.

Dylan raised his eyebrow. "I'm amazed. When I was her age, I was protesting against everything my parents told me to do."

"She thrives in a structured routine." Marcelle closed the door. "Sadie has autism. Her reactions are not the same as a regular teenager in any given situation."

"I see. You called at the gym?"

She put a hand on her forehead. "Ah, yeah. I forgot about that. It was nothing...just...I didn't know whom to call. You already know my parents moved to a retirement condo in Hawaii three years ago and Trudy's out of town. I didn't want to upset them with a call and..."

"Slow down." He put a hand on her arm. Something was wrong; her pupils were dilated, her hands shook as she tried to keep them still. "What's wrong? Are you hurt?"

"Oh no! Nothing like that. Come, I'll show you." She led him inside. "I should've thrown it away, I suppose, but I just couldn't bear to leave Sadie alone in the apartment while I went outside to get rid of it."

Perplexed, he wound his way behind her, past the forest green couch in the living room, the wall-mounted TV, and the vibrant, multicolored carpet that jazzed up the place. Splashes of colors on the wall paintings and prints reflected her love for a lively, bright living space.

"Get rid of what?"

She moved behind the open kitchen counter and bent to open one of the cabinets under the sink. Taking out a cardboard box, she plopped it on the counter. "This."

Dylan opened the box. "What the hell?"

A brown, dead rat, its neck broken, lay over a wad of tissues. Blood pooled from the neck and dotted its fur. "It was outside my apartment door."

Who the hell would do something so vile and vicious? "It what?"

"Someone rang the bell. Sadie found the box. She brought it inside." She gulped air, as a single tear rolled down her cheek. "Thank God, she didn't open it. If she had..."

In one swift move, he enveloped her in a hug. "Shh! Quiet, baby! It's fine. You're all right. Sadie's fine."

She sniffed. "If she had opened it..."

"But she didn't. Everything's fine. What did you tell her was inside the box?"

Marcelle stepped out of his arms and reached for the box of tissues that sat near the basin. "She didn't ask me what was inside." She blew her nose, dumped the tissue into the trash can, and washed her hands over the kitchen sink. "I guess it never crossed her mind to ask." She grabbed the kitchen towel and wiped her hands. "I'm glad she didn't."

"Did you call the police?"

She blinked. "Police? No! I never thought to call them. Why? Do you think I should have? I'm trying hard not to overreact." Marcelle shook her head. "It's probably just a prank, a nasty, cruel one. Sometimes..." She leaned against the counter, making sure to keep her eyes averted from the macabre sight in the box. "Sometimes children do that. It could be someone from the building, or from Sadie's school. Her autism makes her vulnerable. Some kids don't understand...it's possible that one of her classmates got annoyed by something she said and left it here."

Seeing her revulsion, Dylan closed the lid of the box. "Your building has zero security. I just breezed in behind a man who never bothered to ask me who I was before he let me in. There was no guard at the reception desk. I detected no security cameras."

"That must be Mr. Evans. He has been warned many times to be careful, but he keeps forgetting."

"Anyone could've left it on your doorstep. Has anything like this ever happened before?" His mind flashed to the slashed tires of his car. Could these two incidents be connected? She'd been with him that night. He dismissed the notion. He was probably being too paranoid.

"No, never! This is a nice neighborhood. Sure, the security in the building could do with a boost, but the neighbors are nice and everyone looks out for each other."

He mulled over the situation. "We should call the police. Make a complaint."

Marcelle chewed her bottom lip, looking distressed. "If the police come here, Sadie's going to know. Anything like that is bound to upset her and stop the progress she's made so far. It takes her time to adjust to a new routine and environment. She's doing so well, and I would hate to upset her."

"All right. We'll not call the police, but anything like this happens again, you call me. Also, it would help if you talked to someone about boosting the building security." He picked up the box. "I'll go downstairs and get rid of this." He strode away before she could say something. Once downstairs, he walked to the nearest dumpster and threw the box in.

It alarmed him that someone would do something so spiteful and cruel. Knots of tension coiled in his belly. But for now, there was little else he could do except to instruct Marcelle to be more cautious.

Once more, he rang the bell. She opened the door. "I threw it away."

For a moment they both stared at each other. "Coffee?" she asked, her voice hesitant. "Thank you for coming, and for doing...that. I just couldn't gather the nerve to go down with it."

"You're welcome and coffee would be great."

What the hell was he doing? He'd meant to say good-bye and leave. What else was there to do now that she had openly told him she was dating someone else? The thought of someone getting to touch her, to make love to her, brought his blood to a boil—but he forced himself to calm down. He'd no claim over her.

None.

She poured piping hot coffee into a white, ceramic mug and gave it to him. "You're not having any?"

"I had three cups since that...that box came in. Anymore and I won't be able to sleep."

He sat on one of the bar stools that stood against the kitchen counter. "How was your date?" If he could've cut his tongue in half, he would have done so. How the hell did that question slip through his lips?

She cleared her throat and then fiddled with the heart-shaped pendant she wore around her neck. "Umm...actually, it wasn't so great."

He wasn't going to say anything.

Keep your mouth shut. Keep your mouth shut.

He waited another heartbeat. "Why?"

"We went for a picnic. He's a nice guy. Sweet, caring, a few years older than I am."

He took a sip of his coffee, without actually tasting it. It burned like hell. He'd forgotten how hot it was. Dare he ask something else? "So what went wrong?"

"He wasn't you," she said simply.

Time stopped.

Chapter Ten

MJ's stomach rolled. There, she'd said it! And there was no taking back her words. If that date with Craig wasn't enough to give her a jolt, the fact that Dylan was the first person she'd thought to call when she saw that horrible dead rat certainly was an indication of where her heart belonged. Sure, she'd dismissed calling him—and instead gave a call to Trudy who was out of town—but he'd been the one she wanted with her.

And when she did call him, despite their little spat the other day, he'd come right over. What did that say about him? It told her that he cared deeply, unabashedly, without any reserves or pretenses.

It was time to put a stop to her foolishness.

Dylan put his coffee cup down with care. "What do you mean?"

She scowled. It was clear that he was going to make her bleed. "I mean, my heart is stuck on you, isn't it? So I told Craig that I wouldn't be able to see him again."

Within a heartbeat, his arms were around her. "You've made me run in circles. I hope to hell you meant what you just said."

"I may be an idiot from time to time, but I certainly don't repeat my mistakes." She looked into his eyes. What she saw overwhelmed her. Did she deserve such a man? His beauty; his warmth; and his generous, loving nature—it was as if he'd been made just for her. Gently, she cupped his cheek with her hand. "I'm totally mad for you. And if that makes me a rule-breaker or a pariah in social circles, I don't give a damn."

"That's my girl." He chuckled.

She raised her head, her lips inches away from his. Should she say what was on her mind?

"Marcelle?"

Oh, yeah. She'd just go for broke and the consequences be damned.

"I want you to stay the night with me."

Something flashed across his face. Hope? Triumph? Relief? And then his fingers slid inside her hair, and he cupped her head. His lips swooped down on hers. His mouth was hard, hot, and demanding. There was nothing soft or yielding about this kiss; he plundered her mouth with his tongue.

"Would you stay...please?"

Finally, he raised his head. "Sadie?"

"Already sleeping."

"We should go inside."

She should have thought of it, but he was the one who cared enough about her daughter's feelings to remind her. It melted her heart. "Come." With his hand in hers, she led him inside to her room.

How long had it been since she was naked in front of a man? There had been no one serious since Rod, and she had been too caught up in her new life, in Sadie, in her responsibilities to care much if that was a good or bad thing. As she stood in front of Dylan, her hands twitched. She clasped them together in order to quiet their involuntary movements. Yes! She was nervous.

It had been a long time; and this was Dylan. It mattered what he thought of her.

"Marcelle?" His hand caressed her cheek. "Are you sure? I want you badly, but I don't want you to do something you're not ready for."

Was she ready? Darn it, she was! She'd never been ready for anything else in a long time. The heat, the need for him, burned inside her belly. "I'm ready." She had the sudden need to touch him, to explore him.

Her blood churned, sending a trickle of lust down below. As if responding to the hot need inside her, he scooped her in his arms as if she was a bag of feathers. She felt the tension in his muscles as he carried her to the bed.

"I'm going to kiss and lick and suck every inch of your body" he promised, "until you beg for me to stop."

His words caused her to shiver. She put her arms around his neck, making him drop on top of her. "Why don't you start...right now?" Was that her voice, a breathless whisper? Full of need for Dylan?

His lips wandered down her jaw, her neck, and kissed the hollow between her collarbones. Her skin hummed with sensations as he licked and kissed her. Dylan grasped the edge of her blouse, and panic set in.

She was forty-two years old, for heaven's sake. She didn't have the body of a twenty-four year old. Not anymore. Her breasts were no longer perky and upright; her belly and thighs were inundated with stretch marks, although the appearance had improved since her nightly routine of rubbing cocoa butter on her skin; her butt was not a round peach; and her legs had cellulite, although her workouts had helped in that department. What was she thinking, getting into bed with an Adonis like Dylan?

"Stop it," Dylan warned.

"Stop what?"

"Overthinking things."

And before she realized what his intentions were, he ripped her blouse open and tossed it aside.

It pleased her to see his eyes glaze with lust as he gazed down at her body. "You're beautiful."

All the doubts and fears she felt melted away as she recognized that look in his eyes. A man couldn't look at a woman like that and not want her badly enough. Had she been driving herself mad over nothing?

Their hands moved in unison, removing clothes, and throwing them aside. He buried his face in her breasts, licking her delicate nipples until she was all but screaming with delight. As promised, he kissed, licked, and sucked her, taking his time, tasting and savoring each spot as if it was a favorite dessert. Electric jolts seared her body with each touch.

A soft moan escaped her lips. Her hands fisted in his hair and jerked him up, forcing him to meet her lips again. She ran her fingers down his neck, his hard, muscled back, and down to his hips. Her body arched with pleasure as he fit his body against hers.

Putting his elbows down on the bed, he lifted his torso, looking down at her as she gasped. MJ looked sideways as his hand clutched hers. The difference between his peaches and cream complexion and her dark-colored skin was stark, yet they looked so perfect together.

Need and nerves: all her senses awakened and she gave in to the urgent demands of her body. Even as he touched her, she yearned for him. As his hand stroked her, bringing her closer and closer to the edge of that deep, yawning abyss, her body writhed and twisted. His scent, that particular male, citrusy smell, assailed her senses. She ached for that burst of fulfillment, that one, long moment of utter bliss. All other thoughts escaped her mind as she longed for him to free her.

"Dylan!" She breathed his name as her heart lurched. He dove into her and drove her over that crest of desire, her body shuddering, her pulse galloping as she rode the wave of hot passion.

And all the while, his eyes remained fixed on her face—and only when she crossed that peak did he allow himself to ride the torrent of the climax.

He dropped down on her, their bodies sleek with sweat. He was heavy, but she didn't have the energy to ask him to move—she didn't want him to. At least, not yet. It felt wonderful to be pinned under his hard body. For a while, silence reigned in the room as they got their breath back.

Finally, her head stopped swimming long enough to stroke a hand down his arm. "Dylan."

"Hmm?" His voice seemed to come from far away.

"You're squeezing me."

He chuckled and rolled over. Now that he was lying next to her, she felt exposed, conscious again. Marcelle cast a glance around them to see if she could find her torn blouse. Before she could make a move, his hand clutched hers, and he brought their intertwined hands to rest over his heart.

"That was wonderful."

A chuckle escaped her lips. Why was she

doubting herself? It was time for her to stop it. She raised up and propped her chin on her palm, and looked down at his marvelous, glorious body. He was magnificent: all hard planes and angles, muscles that bulged at just the right places, and skin that glowed with the aftermath of incredible sex. She felt that warm tickle in the center of her being, and her skin quivered with anticipation.

She leaned over and kissed him gently on the lips. "Dylan. When you're ready, I am up for round two."

Shocked, his eyes snapped open. "You're going to kill me."

She licked his lower lip with the tip of her tongue. "But you're going to die a happy man, aren't you?"

"Yeah." He groaned. "That's true."

And so it started again.

Chapter Eleven

Dylan went over the notes Kelsey had painstakingly jotted down in the margins of a file for a new client. He added his own feedback about diet and exercise routine. Putting that aside, he delved into the paperwork he'd been neglecting for some time. The gym's license had to be renewed. Two of his treadmills needed to be replaced. He'd already earmarked new machines. It was time to place an order.

An hour later, he'd done his share of the paperwork. A few items had been marked for his manager who was there to oversee the gym. Now, it was time to take care of another small task.

"Is Elijah in there?" he asked the receptionist as he walked into the lobby.

"He came in over an hour ago. Kelsey's with him."

Dylan walked over to the main hall, but Kelsey was there monitoring another client.

"Where's Elijah?"

"He hit the shower five minutes ago."

Perhaps it wasn't a good idea. Maybe he was making too much of a situation that was essentially under control. As he stood outside the shower area, debating his next move, Elijah strode out. A tall, imposing man of six feet four inches, he had an impressive body which he maintained by working out regularly. He was a police officer and had been coming to the gym for over a year.

"Hey, what's up, Dylan?"

Dylan fell into step beside him as Elijah moved to the lockers to remove his bag. "Just wanted to run something by you..."

"Sure."

"A friend of mine had an incident a few days ago. Someone left a box in front of her apartment door. It contained a dead rat."

Elijah swung his bag out. His eyebrows shot up as he stared at Dylan. "A dead rat?"

"Yeah!" Dylan felt foolish. Marcelle had been right. It was probably kids. He shouldn't have said anything, but it felt good to get the take of a professional in this situation. Call him chauvinistic, but he wanted to protect her.

"Did she report it to the police?"

"No. She didn't want to."

Elijah scratched his jaw. "Was there a threatening letter or note that accompanied that dead rat?"

"Nope!"

"Given the fact that she wasn't directly threatened, I don't think the police would be able to do anything even if she filed a report."

"Have you ever seen anything like that in your line of work?"

"Plenty. Could be a pissed-off employer or employee, ex-boyfriend, a neighbor. People are weird." Elijah rubbed his jaw. "If I were you, I'd ask her to be careful, keep the door locked, be cautious when she gets in and out of the building, take notice if anyone tries to follow her around, and maybe take a self-defense class."

"Self-defense class? Isn't that a bit extreme?" Dylan walked Elijah to the door.

"All women should take such classes. It would reduce our work and keep them safe. Would be a good idea for you to start them in this gym. Don't need much equipment for it and you've got plenty of space."

"Yeah?" Dylan nodded, turning the idea over in his head. "I'll think about it."

"And tell your friend that if anything else happens, she should go straight to the police. Most of these incidents don't add up to much. Most likely whoever it was got their anger burned out by this bizarre act, but if it happens again, it could be something serious. A stalker, a psychopath."

"Ok. I'll tell her. Thanks." Dylan turned back, mulling over the idea of self-defense classes. Why not? He'd probably have to do a short course, get the certification, and license. It was something to think about anyway.

But in the meantime, he worried about Marcelle. Sure, she wasn't a helpless woman trapped in a crisis situation. She had guts: guts enough to walk out of a marriage that wasn't working, raise a child with special needs on her own, and make a success of her life, all on her terms—but that didn't mean he shouldn't at least look out for her.

It was surprising how easy his life had slid into her rhythm over the past few days, or perhaps she'd slid into his. Most evenings they went out for a quick coffee, or if she could manage, dinner. He'd dropped by her apartment a few times, but she'd never been to his. Of course, it wasn't easy for her to leave Sadie for the night and he'd never pushed her.

Her daughter came first. That went without saying. He respected her priorities. She wouldn't be the woman she was if she didn't put the needs of her child before his or before their burgeoning relationship. And yes, sure as hell, that is what it was. They were in a relationship, one that involved lunches, dinner, and hot, sweaty sex whenever they could grab a little time alone. *And he couldn't get enough of her.* It wasn't that he was a sex-crazed maniac, but everything about her drove him to that steep, slippery edge of desire from which he wanted to jump off whenever he was with her.

He headed for the main hall. It was time to attend to his clients, and of course, that included Marcelle. Five hours later, he tossed the keys to his manager. "Close up, will you?"

"Hot date?"

"Nothing less would do, my boy!" Dylan walked over to the nearest grocery store. Tonight, he'd finagled an invitation to Marcelle's house for dinner, and the bribe had been his offer to cook. Dylan prided himself on being an enlightened, independent man, and that included his desire to have control over what he put into his mouth. He chalked up a menu that included green beans with lemon and garlic, roast chicken with balsamic bell peppers, and for dessert, a bowl of fresh fruit.

An hour later, he carted over the grocery bags to Marcelle's apartment. Sadie opened the door. It pleased him that her face lit up as she watched him come in. "What did you bring?"

"Dinner."

"Chinese?" Hope floated in her words. He'd discovered that she had a weakness for Chinese food.

"Nope! Even better."

She watched as he dumped the bags on the counter and took out the chicken, potatoes, beans, lemon, and cheese.

"These aren't even cooked."

"And when they're cooked, you'll lick your fingers."

"Argh! That's gross. I would never do that." She shook her head with vehemence. "How long will it take? I'm hungry."

"Where is your mom?"

"She is completing some office work. And then she's going to take a shower. Should I tell her that you're here?"

"No. Why don't we let her finish up? In the meantime, I'll make dinner."

Emotion roiled in her eyes. Interest? Curiosity? "What are you making?"

"Roast chicken. My specialty. Do you want to help me?"

She looked surprised by his offer. "What do I have to do?"

"You could wash and cut the fruit and the beans."

They set to work. Dylan gave her instructions, and even though she was old enough to wield a knife, he watched carefully as she cut the fruit into cubes. Quickly, he put water in a pan and set it on the stove. As the water boiled, he peeled and cut the potatoes. Dylan squeezed the lemons and made the marinade for the chicken. By the time, Marcelle came out, Sadie had set the table for three, the potatoes were boiling, and the fruit was chilling in the fridge in bowls.

"Something smells good in here," Marcelle waltzed into the kitchen, dressed in one of those cotton-soft robes. Her cute button nose crinkled as she sniffed around the stove.

As usual, his heart thumped hard as he cast a glance in her direction. Her face was scrubbed clean of makeup, her hair was wrapped in a towel, turban style, and she was gorgeous.

Good enough to eat!

"Sadie, turn your back. I'm going to kiss your mom."

"Argh!" Sadie turned her back as Marcelle slid her arms up his neck and gave him a soft peck on the lips.

"That wouldn't do at all, especially when I've been slaving over dinner."

"And making my daughter work too, I see."

"And a fine job she did." Dylan stole another kiss. Soft and warm and mushy. He felt her heart slam against her chest as he nipped her bottom lip.

"Are you guys done yet?" Sadie said in a voice that was tinged with exasperation.

"Yes, smarty pants! You can turn around now," he said.

Sadie huffed, turned around, and watched them both with suspicious eyes as if she expected them to go at it right in front of her. Finally, she opened the refrigerator and popped a slice of apple in her mouth. "When is dinner going to be ready?" she whined.

"Ah! A typical teenager. Nothing but food on her mind." Dylan poured the marinade over the chicken. "I was thinking perhaps the three of us could go to the roller-skating rink. Next Sunday would be good if you're all free."

"All of us?" Sadie asked.

"Yes, all of us."

"Can we go, Mom? Please?"

"Sure." Marcelle stared at him as she agreed to her daughter's plea.

"I'm going to go work on my project. Call me when you're finished cooking." Sadie sauntered out, whistling.

Dylan set out the green beans and the salad he'd cut up. "What?" He caught Marcelle staring at him.

She cleared her throat. "I don't know how you've done it, but I've never seen Sadie behave like this with anyone. She actually talks to you. I mean, she treats you like a friend."

"She's a nice kid. I like her. And you've raised her well." He grabbed hold of her hand and raised it to his lips for a kiss.

"She never talked to Rod. Not really! Mostly she slunk out of the room when he was around." She gave Dylan's hand a light squeeze, picked up the salad and the beans, and carried them over to the table.

Dylan debated. He hated to push her, but they'd been together for a week now. "What was he like, your husband? I know he cheated on you, but..."

"You'd like to know more, and I understand." She sat down at the table.

"But not now. Not today. Can we just enjoy a nice dinner and casual conversation over a glass of wine?"

Dylan put the chicken in the oven and pulled out the wine bottle. He popped open the cork. "Sure." He was all for a casual conversation. There was nothing he didn't enjoy doing with Marcelle—even if it was exchanging gym gossip.

As far as he was concerned, life was good and couldn't get any better.

Chapter Twelve

MJ watched her daughter as she roller-skated with panache. "Last year, she worked like a demon for three weeks, falling on her bottom and getting scrapes and cuts, and then suddenly she was like a swan, all grace and speed. It took her a while to learn all these complicated maneuvers, but look at her now."

Dylan leaned on the railing, his eyes following Sadie as she executed a perfect crossover turn. "She's good."

MJ put her hand on his. "I want to thank you for including her. It was sweet of you to offer for her to come along."

Dylan turned to face her. He adjusted her cap. "Oh, yeah! It's a real hardship to enjoy the company of two beautiful women. Sadie's a delight, Marcelle. I like talking to her. She's fun."

How she'd once longed to hear her ex-husband say these words! Dylan had so easily formed a bond with Sadie; whereas, her ex-husband, Sadie's father, couldn't bear to exchange two sentences with her.

"I love her. She's the light of my life." MJ's heart flipped as Sadie whizzed by at top speed, nearly colliding with another skater. At the last minute, both skaters swerved and the crisis was averted. "But I know my daughter. Sometimes she just spouts stuff she shouldn't, especially when she gets into one of her moods."

"Every teenager is entitled to a respectable mood swing." Dylan waved at Sadie as she glided by on one foot.

"You're determined to make it easy, aren't you?"

"And you're determined to make it hard, aren't you?" He matched her tone and voice.

She brushed her hand across his arm. "Sooner or later you're going to want to be with someone who's closer to your age, someone who's not saddled with the responsibility of a teenager..."

"Not that same old ringtone, again, Marcelle. Spare me!" He buried his face in his hands. "Please, I beg you."

Despite herself, she laughed. "Stop it. You're so silly, sometimes."

"But you love me anyway." He butted his body against hers.

"Hmm!" she said noncommittally, as the word "love" sent a sliver of panic up her spine. Perhaps, he found it easy to throw such powerful words in her direction but it wasn't as easy for her. Love was a four-letter word, a dangerous word—and a word that carried meaning and embodied commitment. Once she'd believed love could be simple, but now she knew better. It was fraught with complications and problems, and more often than not, led to disappointment.

He ran a finger down her cheek. "So are you going to tell me about your marriage? Your ex-husband?"

Was she ready to talk about it? She hadn't really relived those memories with anyone. Never needed to. It was enough that she'd left, escaped with her daughter, and made a new life for herself. Telling someone would recapture those moments. But perhaps, she could talk to Dylan. At least, she could try.

"Rod was…handsome, charming, and suave. He just swept me off my feet. We were both young, naïve, and very much in love," she began. Had it been that long ago? More than a decade. Close to two decades, really. "And we were happy. I don't want you to get the impression that I didn't have good times with him. I did. Life was going exactly as we'd planned it, wanted it. Rod had a good job in an investment bank. He was brilliant at his work."

Sadie whizzed by. "Look at me, Mom!" she yelled as she executed a perfect barrel roll.

MJ gave her thumbs up. "We bought a house. I was working. Everything was going great. And then we decided to have a baby. It was the right time. We wanted two. Sadie came along, and for the first few months, everything was great. Of course, the stress of raising a child, the firstborn, was ever present. I quit my job as I wanted to be a stay-at-home mom. Rod was happy with whatever made me happy." She took a deep breath. "Sadie was two when I…when we…Rod and I, realized that something wasn't quite right. She wasn't like the average toddler. She couldn't interact with us the way other kids her age did with their parents. It was…devastating."

"Autism is becoming more and more common among children," he said. When she gave him a curious glance, he shrugged. "I read about it on the internet."

"Rod just couldn't deal with it. I don't know how else to describe it...after the initial diagnosis, he just sort of fell apart. He'd never been an extremely hands-on father, but now, he simply distanced himself from Sadie, from me." All of a sudden MJ felt weighed down. "My entire focus shifted. I was determined to do anything, and everything, to make sure she got the best treatment, the required therapy, and the care and attention she needed to overcome the social and academic issues she faced."

"And the results can be seen." Dylan pointed his hand at Sadie who did a high-five with another skater as they crossed each other. "She's quite well-adjusted for a child with autism."

"She was always high-functioning. Her challenge was social and personal interactions with others, and she has really benefited from therapy. The earlier you start, the better the results. I carted her from one class to another, one teacher to another, one therapist to another, always looking for something more, something better." The heaviness spread to her chest. "I spent hours with her each day, playing, teaching, interacting, and monitoring progress. It's...It's hard to say it, but I did neglect Rod."

"Don't make excuses for him," he shot.

Now that she had opened the dam, the flood was unstoppable. Why hadn't she known that she needed to talk about it with someone other than the therapist? "I'm not making excuses. Rod tried to adjust to the changed family dynamics. Maybe he didn't try hard enough. And I was to blame also. My whole world became Sadie. There was no room for him anymore. The unraveling of our marriage began slowly; there were little hints at first. He came home late from the office, went out at night with his friends, and made excuses to be out of the house on weekends. Later, came the affairs...and finally the beatings."

"He beat you?" Shock coated his words.

"A slap here, or there. A punch in the stomach." Her voice hitched, and then became stable. It was all in the past. She'd moved on. "I ignored him, telling myself that it would get better once Sadie grew older, once she crossed one milestone and then another. Things escalated, until finally one day, I'd had enough. It was the day he hit me on the face. My right eye turned black. I still remember his furious, angry face. His lips peeled back over his teeth." She shuddered at the memory. "I waited until he was fast asleep. Didn't even pack a bag for Sadie and me." MJ took a deep breath and then expelled it slowly. "I sought shelter for Sadie and me at a safe house and we stayed there for several months. The people there were great. Got the counseling Sadie and I needed. Got a job. Filed for divorce. It was messy, difficult, and scary...at first." MJ shook her head at the memories. "But then, everything got better. I eventually quit my job because it was taking me nowhere. And decided it was time to come back home."

For a few long moments, Dylan simply stared at her. Finally, he enveloped her in a big hug. "You're the strongest, most wonderful, and amazing woman I know."

MJ smiled. "It wasn't me being strong. It was me trying to survive and keeping my baby girl, my Sadie, with me."

He held her hand in his firm grasp. "And not everyone can do that."

MJ turned back to watch her daughter glide over the skating floor. It felt right; it felt good to have him there by her side, to share her life, and to relive old memories, no matter how bad they were—but she couldn't help but wonder how long their relationship would last.

Sooner or later, Dylan would go back to his life, and she would be left alone once more, to pick up the pieces as best as she could. *What the heck?* She banished the sad thoughts from her mind. He was here now, with her, and she was going to make the most of this moment.

And such a lovely moment it was too.

Chapter Thirteen

Dylan dumped the mats on the floor, lined them up, and eyed the arrangement critically.

Marcelle paced the floor. "Do we have to do this?"

"I told you, baby, it would help me figure out the best way to teach other women who want to take this class." He'd already applied for the certification and license for self-defense classes. He would have to attend a training class for three months, and then he would become eligible to teach the women who chose to take this course. "You're my guinea pig." He planted a kiss on her forehead. "And such a cute one too."

"I'm just..." She squared her shoulders and caught the gloves he threw in her direction. "Fine. But don't blame me if I land one on your nuts."

"Ouch!" He winced at that image. "Go easy on me."

Marcelle bared her teeth, looking like a cute ninja in the black band around her forehead, the black T-shirt and tights, and the gloves on her hands. "No mercy for you!"

"Yeah, that's that spirit." He bounced on his feet. "Now, see here, how I execute this kick. Raise your leg like that and try to hit me here." He watched as she attempted to kick him. With a swift pivot, he went out of her range. "Good try! Try another!" He pivoted again. "Good one. Try another."

"Will you stop moving around so I can land one on you?" Marcelle hissed.

He loved this woman, but he had no intentions of making things easy for her. "No, you have to catch me first." He darted in, just to tease her and earned a kick on his shin. *So much for being cocky!* "You catch on fast."

She panted. "I'm a quick study."

"Look here now." He showed her a few fast jabs and thrusts. "Someone comes at you. Bam bam bam! It'll be over in a few minutes."

"And what if he's bigger and meaner than I am?"

"Learning self-defense will give you confidence if you have to face a stalker or an attacker, but your first move should be to get yourself to a safe place." He bounced around a bit. "I hope to God you don't actually have to fight someone one day, but if you do, you won't be completely helpless."

"I'm not helpless." She aimed a jab at his face. He grabbed her hand, pulled, and she landed right on top of him as they toppled over.

"Suddenly, I'm enjoying this session more and more." He ran a hand up her back and rested it on the nape of her neck. Desire coiled in his gut, slammed into his heart.

"You have a one-track mind."

She was so beautiful. He lifted his head to kiss her on the lips. As always, the taste of her, the touch of her, everything about her, sent his senses reeling. His yearning for her never ended. He always wanted more. He trailed kisses down her jaw and then with a groan, he pulled her closer, reveling in the musky scent that enveloped her.

It was simply impossible for him to keep

his passion for her under control when she was around him. She was like a drug, and he was her powerless addict.

Always before, their love making had been slow, tender, and gentle. Today, it was different. His need for her was strong, unbearably so. He wanted her now. Quick and hard. As his tongue thrust inside her mouth, tasting, touching, and devouring, he pulled her T-shirt over her head and made quick work of her bra. Thank God, the clasp was in the front, because he didn't want to waste a second when he could be wrapped around her heat. The rest of her clothes followed. With delight, he ran a hand up her smooth back to the side of her breasts.

Her fingers dug into his shoulders and glided up his neck. She buried them in his hair, pressing herself closer to him, almost as if she had an urge to burrow deep inside him. A soft sigh escaped her lips as he moved his own down her jaw. With a swift move, he turned, so that she was under him.

Her lips lifted in a bright smile. "I like this maneuver. You've got to do that more often." Then she cleared her throat, her eyes danced with merriment. "Are you going to do me with all your clothes on?"

He didn't have the time or inclination to

respond. He just wanted her. Now. He dove into his pocket and thanked his lucky stars that he had the good sense to slip the foiled packet there, not that he'd planned for what they were doing right then to happen. He tore the wrapper and clumsily slid on the protection, not even bothering to slip his track pants or his sleeveless T-shirt right off...all amidst her teasing banter. But he couldn't care less. He'd have her hollering his name in a matter of seconds. He chuckled at the thought.

He could never have enough of her. Her body was all soft, feminine, and curvy. Her legs, so smooth and strong, her belly slightly rounded, and those magnificent breasts that he couldn't get enough of; she was a goddess. Dylan put his palms on either side of her on the mat, his body poised above her. He bent his head and took her erect nipple in his mouth. Her moan of delight sent shivers down his belly. He felt his stomach tighten as she arched under him. She appeared to be delirious with raging desire. He felt the beat of her heart, heard her moan as he kissed and sucked. Her legs opened, as if she couldn't wait for him to ravish her.

All his senses were focused on how he felt with her naked body entwined with his. He raised his head, and his hands moved to feel the soft, smooth weight of her warm breasts, then trailed down her ribcage to her belly. A tremor shook her body as she gasped his name, again and again. Several expressions flitted across her face as his finger trailed a path down her belly button to the curls at the juncture of her thighs. She was wet when he slipped his finger inside her. Her body arched as he pleasured her. He wanted to leave her breathless, weak, begging for more.

As the orgasm ripped through her, rendering her helpless, she shuddered under him. Unable to restrain himself any longer, he groaned loudly as he lifted her hips and drove himself inside her hot, wet center. His eyes remained fixed on her, watching the swirl of emotions on her face. His body, hot with desire, slick with sweat, quivered as he reveled in her warmth. She wrapped her legs around him, pushing her hips up and down in a rhythm that drove him crazy.

The wave of need spun through, crested and peaked. He moaned, muttered her name, and emptied himself inside her.

They lay silent and still, both of them lost in the ecstasy of the moment.

"Some self-defense lesson," she said.

Dylan chuckled. He wasn't sure if he could move, or breathe, or stand. Damn it! Did he just make hot, passionate love to Marcelle in his gym? Thank God, it had been near closing time. What if someone walked in? With that thought in his head, he rolled off her, sat, and caught his breath. He pulled out her bra from under his leg and handed it over. She snatched it from him, and scrambled around for her other clothes. She put them on hastily.

"We just had fast, furious sex on the gym floor. That's so…" She appeared lost for words.

He tipped her chin up so she could look directly at him. "Hot? Amazing? Fulfilling?"

"Yes, yes, and yes." She gave him one of her slow, sweet smiles. "But I've never done something like that before."

He put an arm around her shoulders and squeezed her tightly, then clasped her hand in his as they went out of the door. The gym was quiet, eerily so. It was late. "Come on, let's take a shower, and then I'll drop you home."

He whistled as he sauntered to the men's room. As far as he was concerned, life couldn't get any better than this. Dylan knew he was falling in love with Marcelle. It was a tumble he was willing to take, wanted to take. Sure, Marcelle wasn't quite there yet. She had deep feelings for him, he could tell—but she wasn't as ready yet to admit that she loved him back.

It was something he would have to work on. Dylan had never been scared to take on a challenge. Marcelle might not realize it, but he was nudging her along to exactly where he wanted her to be—and that was in his arms.

Forever.

Chapter Fourteen

MJ made a plate of hors d'oeuvre and put it on the counter. Dylan was coming over later, and after drinks, they'd go out for dinner. The sitter was coming to stay with Sadie. She adjusted the strap of her dress and went over to pick up the phone as it rang.

"Hello."

"MJ, hi. It's Leslie."

To her complete annoyance, her mind went blank. "Leslie?"

"How are you? And Sadie?"

Good manners took over despite the fluster in her heart. This was one of her best friends. There was a time when there was little in MJ's life that Leslie didn't know about. But suddenly, she felt self-conscious, even scared. "Fine. Great. And you?"

"The job's going quite well." Leslie's voice was light, breezy. "I just returned from a trip to Vancouver. Beautiful place, by the way. Hardly saw much as we were busy with conferences and meetings, but I did manage to see some of the local sights one evening."

MJ sucked in a deep breath of air. "That's great. Wonderful."

"So I heard you're dating my brother?"

Damn! This is awkward.

Mentally, she cursed Dylan. "Yeah! Umm..."

Luckily, Leslie was always the one who did most of the talking in any conversation. "He told me. Said how you were absolutely hung up on the age difference between you two. It's crazy, I told him." She chuckled. "In this day and age, who cares! Celebrities do it all the time...what's the name of that couple? Tina Turner and Ervin or Erwin Bach, is it?

MJ squeezed her eyes shut. "It's Erwin." She cleared her suddenly dry and itchy throat. "Tina Turner's new husband is Erwin." She wished the floor would magically open and swallow her up.

"Anyway, I told Dylan I would give you a

call and put you at ease."

"Right." Anger snaked into the pit of her stomach. Couldn't he at least have warned her? And what else had he discussed with his sister?

"I think it's absolutely terrific. Dylan was always mature for his age, you know what I mean? All well-mannered, well-behaved." She chuckled. "What am I saying? You were right there when he was growing up."

Good lord. What could she say in response to that? She was a frequent visitor at the McCoy's residence when she was growing up. MJ felt the bead of perspiration slowly making a trek down her forehead.

"Our mom never had any trouble with him, I can tell you that. But then again, you already know that."

MJ closed her eyes in mortification. What the hell was she supposed to say? "So, when are you coming back home for a visit?"

"Next month, maybe. Now that Dylan has told me all about the two of you, I'm dying to come and spend a couple of days with you both. Maybe I'll fly down for a weekend." Leslie's voice was laced with enthusiasm. "That would be awesome."

"Yes, awesome," MJ repeated. This was Leslie. Her friend. Why couldn't she think of something to say?

"So anyway, I just wanted to say hi, and all that. I'll see you soon."

"Right. Bye."

MJ put the phone down, and plopped on the stool. What the hell? Her heart was racing, and she was sweating. If Dylan had warned her that he'd talked to his sister, she might have been more prepared to hold up her end of the conversation. And what was the need to discuss their relationship with Leslie?

In time, of course, she might have talked to Leslie, discussed her relationship with Dylan. They exchanged phone calls; MJ, Trudy, and Leslie were thick as thieves. But to have this drop down on her head without warning, without any preparation, just floored her. Anger burned, slowly and steadily, in her gut. She'd sounded like a fool, she knew.

The doorbell rang. She heard Sadie's footsteps as she went to open the door, and her warm greeting as she led Dylan in.

"How did your science project go?" Dylan asked Sadie.

"A minus," she said.

"Good job."

"It could've been better if I'd put in more effort. I'm going to finish my homework."

Dylan walked into the kitchen. "That girl works too damn hard. At her age, I was scraping by with Bs."

"Not according to your sister. Apparently you were a model child." The anger she'd been trying to control spewed.

"Leslie called?" He dumped his jacket on a stool, and bent to kiss her on the cheek. "You look smashing."

She smoothed her dress, a pretty red number that she'd picked up for tonight's dinner. It had seemed like a good idea at that time: an unusual splurge to mark the five months they'd been dating. And the results of her diet and exercise regime had really begun to kick in over the last few weeks; it showed, especially the way she looked in that dress. What had she been thinking? MJ stood. "Don't you think it would have been a good idea to give me some warning that Leslie was going to call?"

"She did say something to that effect. I just talked to her last night. That woman sure doesn't waste any time." He sat on the stool adjacent to her, reached for a cracker on the table, and popped it into his mouth.

His nonchalant behavior gave the simmering fire of rage a boost. "Perhaps this doesn't mean anything to you, Dylan, but I don't appreciate being the butt of any jokes."

His eyes narrowed. "Leslie made fun of you?"

MJ waved her hand. "Of course not. She was very...nice, very understanding...of our situation. Said how you were always too mature, and..."

"And?"

MJ put her hand on her hip. "Well, apparently, she doesn't think it's a big deal that we're going out. This age difference doesn't bother her."

"Why would it bother her?" He lifted one shoulder. "Leslie's cool!"

"Well, I'm not cool." Her temper snapped. "I'm not cool with people talking about us."

"Leslie is not 'people.' She's my sister, and it might surprise you, but I do talk to her about my girlfriends on occasion. We're close, and I thought she was your friend also. Your best friend, in fact." His words contained a little bite, just the bare hint of it.

"I don't want anyone to know about us. That makes this thing...too real." She waved a hand. "And I'm not sure..."

The snap of anger in his eyes made her rethink her words. He stood, slowly, and faced her. "Real? What's not real about this relationship?"

"You know what I mean."

"Do I?" Dylan cocked an eyebrow, his stare icy.

She wasn't going to fight this battle sitting down. So incensed was she, that she struggled to get on her feet. "It's not going to last, all right. You're much younger than I am. How long are we supposed to stay together? Nine months? A year? Maybe two? It's not as if we have a future together."

"So what am I? A fling? A way to pass time until you find someone else? Someone who fits the age range to be with you?"

"Don't be silly. I just don't want you wasting time with someone you can't have forever with."

"I already have someone I want to spend the rest of my life with. And that someone is you. But instead of concentrating on being with me and loving me, you're trying to get rid of me, because you think I'm not old enough to love you."

"You're not thinking this through. What about kids?" she demanded. "In a few years I won't be able to have any. What if you want children one day?"

Dylan paced the floor, and MJ watched as he made his way back and forth. "Would it make sense for me to have children with a woman I don't love? Or to let you go simply because I may want to have kids one day?" he asked. "There's still enough time for you and me to have kids if we want to." He stopped in front of her. "And in case you didn't know this, you're *not* old. And adoption is always an option, if that's what we both wanted."

She sputtered. "You're...you're so blasé."

"And you're so anal," he retorted. He began pacing again.

How had this thing turned around so that it was her fault? He was the one who'd embarrassed her by talking to Leslie about her. He was the one who had nudged, pushed, and shoved her until she'd given in and started something that was bound to end in disaster. But still, she was the one being painted as the bad guy here.

I don't like it. No sir! And she wasn't going to take this kind of crap in her own house.

"I think you'd better leave." She pointed at the door, fighting the tears that threatened to spill. She wasn't going to make a fool of herself in front of him.

Don't you dare cry like a baby, darn it.

She wanted him out of the house. "Neither of us is capable of having a rational conversation right now, and it's better to end it now so we can remain friends."

Dylan banged his hand on the counter. "I've had it with this nonsense, Marcelle. What will it take to convince you that I love you, that our relationship is more important to me than any I've ever had before?" He raked his fingers through his hair. "I can't guarantee the future, but I can guarantee that I'll love you to the best of my ability. But if you're determined to see it as something that doesn't have a future, then you're the one nipping this in the bud." He rubbed his brow as if trying to soothe away a headache. "I can't fight these crazy notions that you've given birth to. You, and only you, are responsible for making our relationship appear trashy, unworthy of any significance. And I won't have it anymore. I want it all: your love, your commitment, and your respect. I will not settle for less, Marcelle."

He reached out and pulled her to him, then gave her a rough, hard kiss, a kiss that made her almost forget what they were arguing about. MJ groaned, and just when she was about to wrap her arms around his neck, he released her.

"Remember that when you're in bed tonight." His voice was tight, hard; his eyes were cold. "And think about all the other nights of good loving you're depriving us of." Dylan picked up his jacket and strode out.

MJ collapsed on the stool and burst into tears.

She was missing him already.

Chapter Fifteen

It had been a week since their fight. A week and two days, but who was counting? MJ tapped her finger on the counter. As usual, her gaze flitted to the phone. She wasn't going to call. She wasn't. She wasn't.

Her affair with Dylan wouldn't have lasted for long, anyway. He was too young to make a lifelong commitment to her. At some point, he would've wanted more: kids, a wife who was better suited to him. She wasn't the one, and she never could be. It would have ended sooner or later—and sooner was better, as far as she was concerned.

"So are you coming with me?" Trudy

came out of the powder room where she'd gone to freshen up. She was going to see a movie with a bunch of friends, and wanted MJ to come along.

"I didn't call the sitter, and Sadie will be home soon." She'd gone with a group of girls to the mall, and one of the girls' mothers was going to drop her off.

Trudy picked up her purse. "MJ, you've been moping around the house for a week now. It's time to either get over him, or call him back."

"Why should I call him? It was his fault."

Trudy eyed her. "I'm not sure if you've reached that stage where I'm supposed to tell you the truth? Or if you just want me to hear you trash him?"

"What are you talking about?" MJ made an effort to focus on her friend.

"I mean, it wasn't really Dylan's fault now, was it? All he did was talk to his sister, much the same way you talk to me. And may I remind you that you've always discussed your relationships with Leslie. So how is this any different?"

"This is way different," she argued. "He told Leslie to call me."

"So what if he did? His intention was to make you feel good, confident, to get that seal of approval that you're so desperately seeking from others, when all you need to do is to accept him in your heart."

"I had accepted him," she argued.

Trudy primped her already perfect hair. "You should've already made peace with the fact that you're attracted to him, but you haven't…or haven't accepted the fact that you're completely in love with him."

MJ jumped up from the couch. "I'm not in love."

Trudy put a hand on her shoulder. "You're absolutely in love with him, and that scares the bejesus out of you."

MJ looked away. "It's not that easy," she muttered. Why couldn't anyone understand her?

"All I' m saying is that Dylan cares about you, probably even loves you. And guys like that don't come around often. So he's not a perfect match for you age-wise. Does age really matter? No one is going to be made-to-order. If it's not the age, it's the race, or his job, or his family, or his friends. If you get so hung up on one particular thing, you're never going to find someone."

"I don't want to find someone. No one seems to have noticed, but I was doing quite well on my own," she muttered. It wasn't easy to take advice, especially if she didn't like what she was hearing.

"Your choice, MJ. But consider this; if

Dylan was older than you, and he'd talked to his sister about you, would you have been flattered or insulted that you mattered enough for him to tell his sister about you?" She paused, letting her words settle in.

MJ considered. Would her response to this situation have been different if this age issue wasn't there? MJ hated soul-searching because it often led to finding answers one didn't like. And if she was to be honest, she didn't like what her heart was telling her.

Damn Dylan! Why did he have to come into my life and complicate everything?

Trudy checked her watch. "I must leave now. Think about what I said, MJ." With a quick wave she was off, leaving MJ to ponder her actions and her reasons for them. Was she afraid to admit that she'd fallen in love with Dylan? Had she really been looking for an excuse to end things simply because she was scared that it wouldn't last longer?

Arrrgh! Why was her life so complicated?

If it was simple, what I'm feeling for Dylan wouldn't be love.

For a long time, MJ sat on the couch, looking into the depths of her heart for answers. Two hours later, the doorbell rang and kept on ringing as if someone had put their hand on it and had forgotten to remove it. "I'm coming." She hurried out, wondering who it could be. Sadie wouldn't ring the bell like that.

To her consternation, it was Sadie, and she was crying as she pointed at the door, her finger still on the bell. MJ moved her daughter's finger, enveloped her in a big hug even as she took in the state of her door. Someone had taken a can of red paint and scrawled abusive words on the door and the adjoining walls.

Sadie's howls brought the neighbors out. A couple in their seventies, the Murphys, recovered from their shock quickly. The woman shuffled forward. "Go on, dear, go back inside." She shooed MJ and Sadie inside their apartment. The elderly woman gestured towards her husband. "Greg, you need to call the police."

"Who would do that, Mom? Who would do that?" Sadie kept chanting as tears poured down her cheeks.

MJ hugged her daughter as she led her into her bedroom. It took her a while to calm Sadie down. Almost an hour later, Sadie lay on the twin-sized bed, her breathing even as she slept. When MJ went back outside, it touched her to see that the neighbors were waiting in her living room. "The police are on their way,"

Mrs. Murphy assured her. "Want me to make some tea for you, dear?"

"No. Thank you." MJ went to answer the doorbell. Two uniformed policemen stood outside, surveying the nasty handiwork. "Are you all right, ma'am?"

"Yes." She welcomed them inside.

"We live in the apartment next door." Mrs. Murphy introduced herself. "When Sadie started crying, we were watching TV and came outside to see what the commotion was all about." She frowned. "This is a nice building. Nothing like this has ever happened before. Of course, I've been telling the superintendent to increase the security. Anyone can come and go as they please without so much as signing a register."

"My neighbors," MJ explained to the police. Her head was spinning. It would take Sadie days to get over this ordeal. Thank God, she hadn't come across the perpetrator while he was busy decorating their wall and door. "They were quite helpful."

One of the police officers, a middle-aged, portly man turned towards Mrs. Murphy. "Ma'am, why don't you and your husband go to your apartment? We'll come by shortly to record your statements."

The police took their time. They asked

questions, took pictures of the outside to include in their report, and even took statements from the neighbors. MJ didn't allow them access to her daughter, knowing it would induce fresh hysterics from the child. She did promise them that she would talk to Sadie and if there was any relevant information, she would call the police and give it to them. She also gave them a detailed account of the dead rat she'd found outside her doorstep weeks ago.

"We'll look into it, ma'am," one of them promised when he left. "This is a clear case of harassment. It could be kids playing pranks, of course, but we can't dismiss the possibility that someone may intend to harm you. We'll ask the residents if any of them saw a stranger enter or leave the building." He jotted down some notes on his pad. "An interview with the superintendent of the building will be scheduled. In the meantime, we want you to keep your door locked at all times. Before opening it, check to make sure that you know the visitor. It might be advisable to accompany your daughter to and from school and her activities for a while."

"Thank you." MJ followed them outside and watched them leave. Finally, she took a moment to study the horrible words painted in a crude, untidy handwriting. The person who did this was full of malice and resentment. It had been a crime of passion, and not a prank.

She went inside and closed the door behind her. Whoever did this would pay one day, she vowed as she walked to her daughter's room. Her heart clenched when she heard Sadie's sobs. They both wouldn't be getting much sleep that night. MJ swore that one day she'd make sure that the culprit suffered the consequences of his actions.

Chapter Sixteen

Rod reviewed the analysis report his team had sent over. As he'd predicted, one of the new companies he'd earmarked as a potential profitable investor was doing quite well.

A clear three hundred thousand dollar profit for my client, exactly as I'd anticipated.

He tapped a pen on the table as he mentally calculated his commission. His cell phone rang. He looked at the display, not sure if he wanted to receive any calls just now. When he saw the name, he picked up the call. "Yes, Sondra." He knew his tone was cold, frosty.

"Rod?" She sounded breathless, a little ill

at ease. "Just wanted to know when you're coming back."

He leaned back. Sondra was his assistant, and his current girlfriend. Ex-girlfriend, he reminded himself. Why couldn't she get the message that he wasn't interested anymore? It had been a bad idea for him to get involved with her. He was done with messing around.

"I'll be back in a week. My work here will be finished soon," he said curtly.

"All right," she hesitated, clearly sensing that he didn't intend to talk much. "Rod..." she started to say something and then stopped.

"I'll see you back at the office." He disconnected the call. No use telling Sondra to lose his cell phone number; he'd just have to change it. He mentally noted that he needed to call the cell phone company to request a new number, and better yet, request that they block Sondra's.

Irritated by the call, Rod pushed the cell phone to the side. He stood and stretched as he walked over to the mirror on the cabinet door. As he ran a hand over his jaw, Rod replayed the conversation with Sondra. She'd sounded sad, even a little bit scared and lonely. He hated clingy women. Why the hell couldn't she understand that he didn't want her anymore? For a while it had been good to hang out with a woman who was so much younger. And there was no denying that the sex had been great, but then, she wasn't MJ.

Rod wasn't ashamed to admit that he was still hung up on his ex-wife. MJ had been the love of his life. He was devoted to her. She'd mattered to him, and their life had been perfect up until the day Sadie arrived. Perhaps, if their child had been normal, things would have worked out—but Sadie's condition demanded too much of MJ's time and effort. Sadie was the reason their marriage fell apart. Ironic, considering that children were usually the glue that held a marriage together.

Still, he shouldn't have hit her. Not once. Not ever. He didn't mind admitting that he hated himself for it. Perhaps, if she had been more attentive to his needs, more willing to delegate the responsibility of their child to a nanny as he'd wanted her to, he wouldn't have become as frustrated with the conditions at home.

His affairs had been the result of deep loneliness. He'd wanted, no needed, MJ's time and attention. Yet she'd been too busy lavishing it all on Sadie, while he came home to a wife who was too exhausted to even sit and make conversation with him after her long, tiring day with a demanding child.

But this was all water under the bridge now. He'd made mistakes, as had she. It was time to start anew. He'd set things in motion, and MJ was going to be back in his arms soon enough. He'd also made plans for Sadie. There was a wonderful residential school for children like her in Chicago. He'd already talked to one of the directors of the school, a new client of his. She would get excellent care there. The teachers were all trained in special needs and would provide the treatment and therapy Sadie needed to flourish. She could come home for the holidays. They would be like a real family again. Maybe he would take MJ for a little holiday. Europe, he thought. The south of France was a romantic destination, and he knew MJ would love it.

Things would work out. Rod was ready to make a new beginning with MJ. He should've gone with her to the therapist when she begged him to, and he should've never let her leave. But now he was willing to do anything to win her back. And by now, she was probably thinking along the same lines.

Rod flexed his muscles, happy to note

that his body was lean and fit due to the rigorous exercise regime he'd been following for the past two years. He knew his khaki-colored skin glowed with health. He knew he was still an attractive man, and there was no shortage of women who paid him attention. But in his heart, Rod was a one-woman man—and that woman was MJ.

As far as he was concerned, MJ was meant to be with him. He was ready to take her back in, and soon, things would be on track—exactly as he'd envisioned.

Chapter Seventeen

Dylan parked his car and walked towards his gym. He wasn't really needed here tonight. Kelsey was handling his clients for the two days that he'd taken off to sort through the mess that was his life. Tired of sitting around and brooding, he'd gone to Philadelphia to visit an old college buddy. Hoping that the distance would give him the much-needed perspective, he'd stayed with his friend and done what all single men did on vacation; hit the clubs, drank too much, and slept very little.

Not that it did me any good.

While it had been nice to hang out with his friend, Dylan had to admit that the trip hadn't cured him of the heartache that was his constant companion even since that fateful night at Marcelle's house. What would it do for him to stop thinking about her? Stop obsessing about her? It wasn't as if there weren't other willing women who were eager to fill her place—yet what could he do if his heart was stuck on her?

But Dylan was done with taking any more shit from her. She couldn't just discard him anytime she chose, simply because it was hard for her to accept their age difference. He was tired of that same old tune. As he'd told her, it was everything or nothing.

"Dylan, you're back early. We weren't expecting you until tomorrow morning," his manager said as he walked inside. As always, the bustling activity in the gym calmed him down. At this time of the evening, people came in from their offices and the gym was packed. Perhaps, he could relieve Kelsey and attend to the rest of his clients.

"Just wanted to pop in to see you all," he said as he strode past reception.

"What's the hurry?" his manager gestured towards the slips of paper on the counter. "Here's a list of messages that were left for you while you were away.

Marcelle called twice."

"Marcelle?" He turned back. What did she want now? His heart pounded as he picked up the slips from the counter.

"She didn't come in yesterday and said she might not be in for the next few days."

Why hadn't she called on his cell? Belatedly, he remembered that he'd turned it off and tossed it inside his bag because he'd wanted to switch off from everything for a couple of days.

The messages didn't release the tension that knotted in his belly. She had only asked him to call her back. "Did she say why she couldn't come in?"

"No." The manager nodded his head. "The supplier called about the new machines you ordered. When would you like the delivery?" He reached for the clipboard and handed it to Dylan. "And we've gotten two new applicants for the gym. You need to approve their memberships...Hey, I thought you were coming in?"

Dylan jogged out of the gym. "Something came up. I'll be in tomorrow."

Marcelle's message had thrown him off kilter. Should he call her back? Or would it be a good idea to pay her a visit? Of course, he could make her wait. Let her stew as he'd been stewing for the past few days. She couldn't just lift a finger and expect him to come running; he had his pride. He plopped into the car and drummed his fingers on the steering wheel, contemplating what should be his next move. With a flick of his wrist he started the SUV and drove towards his apartment.

Screw it!

He was going to see what she wanted. Without further thought, he made a sharp U-turn, tires screeching, mentally crossing his fingers, hoping that he wouldn't hear the dreaded sirens of a patrolman behind him. The last thing he needed was a ticket for a traffic violation and a delay from getting to Marcelle. And if all she had to offer was the same old gibberish, he would never visit her again. It would break his heart, sure—but it was better to sever all ties with her and make a clean start.

He finally reached her building and parked his vehicle. He shook his head when he saw that the main door had been left ajar, and Mr. Evans was nowhere to be found. Dylan jogged up to Marcelle's apartment, ignoring the elevator, since a quick glance at the external control panel revealed that the elevator car was on the top floor. He reasoned that he would get to her apartment faster if he took the stairs .

He took the steps two, sometimes three at a time, aware of the adrenaline coursing through his body. When he got to Marcelle's floor, he raced to the door and rang the buzzer.

No answer.

Perhaps she wasn't home.

He checked his watch. It was seven-fifteen. If she wasn't at the gym, she should be home—unless of course she was on a date with someone. Jealousy reared its ugly head, but he squashed down the nasty feeling. He'd no claim over her. Maybe she'd already moved on, while he was bumbling along trying to find his bearing.

Dylan turned back and took the stairs. He made it down in record time and within seconds he was back behind the steering wheel again. Something niggled at the back of his mind, but he ignored it and switched on the engine. The niggling feeling didn't let go of the grip it had on him. He switched off the engine. He'd come all this way, he figured he might as well see this through. He slid out of the car and strode towards the building for the second time that night. When one of the tenants buzzed in a pizza delivery guy, he slipped in casually behind him. The delivery guy veered left without a backwards glance, and Dylan breathed a sigh of relief.

He watched as the elevator's doors slid open and a giggling couple, perhaps in their late teens, stepped out into the lobby. Judging by the smeared lipstick on the guy's face, Dylan surmised that they'd spent the few moments in the enclosed space getting their groove on. They, too, didn't spare Dylan a moment's notice. Security was really the pits in this building. Dylan decided to take the recently vacated elevator. As the door slid closed, he caught a glimpse of the guy grabbing the young woman's butt cheek. Dylan shook his head. It never ceased to amaze him how brazen teenagers had become.

As the elevator slid upwards, he once again questioned his sanity. Why was he worrying over a woman who obviously didn't want him, or didn't love him, for that matter? What if she wasn't there? Maybe he could write a message and slide it in under her door. Of course, he didn't have a pen or paper on him so it would be hard to write something.

In front of Marcelle's apartment, his finger hovered an inch above the buzzer. Should he? Dare he?

Forget it!

He turned to go back. Voices that filtered in through the thin door stopped him in his tracks. Whom was she talking to inside? He could make out her voice and the voice of a man. Another man? Had she already moved on? Dylan resisted the hot desire to smash his fist against the door. He wouldn't make a fool of himself. If she had found someone else, he'd have no right to interfere. It was her life, and she deserved happiness. He was man enough to walk away and leave her alone, to find and love someone whom she figured she deserved. He turned and hustled away.

He really should go and work off his frustration in the gym. But wait. Something about the loud tenor of the voices made him make an about-face and hurry to the door. When he first heard the voices, he was too busy thinking that another man was with MJ, and not thinking about the tone of the man's voice. Something didn't feel right. He hit the buzzer once. Twice. He strained his ears to make out what was going on. The voices sounded muffled. He'd better ring that buzzer again. Or better yet, he should bust through the damn door.

A sharp scream made up his mind much faster than he'd planned.

It was Marcelle.

And she was in trouble.

Chapter Eighteen

Seeing him at her door, out of the blue, had taken MJ aback. The shock of the encounter made her usher him inside. Since the day of their divorce, she and Rod hadn't had any contact, except to exchange papers through their respective lawyers. Rod had neither shown any interest in claiming joint custody for their daughter, nor had he wanted any visitation rights. He just wasn't concerned about Sadie. And MJ sure as hell wasn't concerned about him. Not after the abuse he'd meted out to her.

"Sadie's not home." Had he come to his senses and realized that he needed to see their daughter on occasion and maintain some semblance of a father-daughter relationship? Hope flared in MJ's heart. Could Rod finally be ready to become a parent?

"I came to see you."

He looked leaner. But it suited him. Rod was always a handsome man and made an effort to look good.

Too bad he couldn't give that much time and effort to our only child.

"Why?"

"It's been a long time, MJ. Aren't you going to invite me to sit?" His voice was warm, sweet.

"No."

He ignored her and took a seat on the couch, leaving her standing. She had no time for this. If he couldn't be bothered about Sadie, he had no place in her life. "What do you want?"

He flashed a familiar smile. "I want you." He raised his hand to stop her from answering him. "And I've realized that I was wrong not to understand the pressure you were under. Sadie wasn't an easy child, and I should've been there to help you, support you. Instead, I got too busy with my work and failed to be there for you."

To say that MJ was in shock was an absolute understatement. Had he lost his mind? She ignored the buzzer as someone pressed the bell at the door. "What are you saying?"

Rod stood up quickly, came forward, and took her hands in his firm grasp. "I've come to my senses now. You're the only one I have ever loved. There is no other. And I still love you. Without you, I'm lost."

MJ was repulsed. She pulled her hand away. This was too unexpected. Crazy. Mad. "I'm…sorry, Rod…I…"

"You don't need to be sorry. I take full responsibility for the failure of our marriage. And I've a solution to make everything all right again, back to the way it was before Sadie was born."

"Before she was born?"

"There's this great residential school for children with special needs, and I have already talked to the director and asked him to reserve a place for Sadie in the coming academic year." Rod gave her a smile, a smile she knew he used to put potential clients at ease, but she knew better. "They have well-trained teachers and staff who take care of children like her. She would get the best care, best support, and of course, she would be able to come home for holidays and be with us."

MJ couldn't wait to get Rod out of her

home and out of Sadie's and her life for good. "Have you gone mad? What makes you think I'll dump my child in a residential school so I could be with you?"

His nostrils flared. Anger roiled in his eyes.

And in that moment, MJ learned something about herself. She wasn't afraid of him anymore. Wasn't afraid of what he could do to her, now that he was angry. She saw the fire in his eyes, and a flash of memory came over her. After the last beating he'd given her, it took her body several days, weeks really, to heal.

She took a calming breath.

"Sadie's nearly grown, MJ. You don't need to devote every second of your life to her anymore."

"I want to take care of her, to be with her when she needs me." MJ should've been feeling frustrated, scared even, but she took a deep breath, and then released it slowly through her lips.

Rod would never change. How could she have ever felt that the failure of their marriage was mostly her fault? He was a selfish ass, and always would remain so. She fought to keep the anger out of her voice. "You wouldn't understand. You never did. But Sadie and I are happy. We've made a life without you. I don't know why you'd think that I might be interested in resuming our relationship, because I've moved on."

"So you would rather be with that jerk who runs a gym, or that lawyer guy than be with the man whom you promised to love and obey till death do us part?"

Her blood ran cold. How dare he keep tabs on her? "How do you know about Dylan and Craig? Have you been following me?" Comprehension dawned; the pieces were finally falling into place. "Oh my God! Were you the one who sent that dead rat? You sick bastard!" she was steamed, not unlike the pressure on the magma chamber far beneath the earth's surface, which builds up. "Did you deface my apartment door?" Her heart pounded heavily against her chest, her body tensed. Even as she waited for Rod to respond, she knew he was the one who'd done the cruel acts. All because he wanted to hurt her and her daughter.

He sneered. "I'm trying to save you from your own folly, MJ. What are people going to say when they hear that you're dating a man so much younger than you? Your actions positively reek of desperation."

How could she have ever thought that she was in love with this man, this monster? How could she have spent years of her life trying to please him? He was a waste of time then—and he was a waste of time now. She marched up to him, her hands on her hips. "The stupid, brainless tactics you employed traumatized my daughter. I ought to call the police and turn you in."

His eyes bulged with rage. He curled his upper lip. "Jeez! You're a crazy bitch."

"What did you call me? Get the hell out of my house!"

Rod's backhand caught her across her cheek and lips.

She screamed, more out of outrage than fear.

She was never going to be afraid of Rod again.

As she staggered back, she could taste blood from the cut on her lip in her mouth.

This is the limit!

She wasn't going to be his punching bag anymore. Those days were well past her. The years of abuse she'd suffered at his hands flashed across her mind. He would pay for it now.

And he would pay for the tears her daughter had shed over his senseless, vicious act of vandalism.

As God was her witness, Rod was going to pay for it.

Now.

She wasn't the same helpless woman he'd thrashed around whenever the urge struck him.

She was smart, intelligent, and capable of protecting herself and her child.

And she also had the benefit of the self-defense classes she had been attending for the last few months.

A deadly calm enveloped her.

And then she released it.

Her power.

Her strength.

Her rage.

She was a Vesuvian eruption, ejecting hot, viscous lava. With full force, she leapt forward and landed a punch in Rod's gut. He yelled, tried to grab her hand, but he wasn't fast enough; she'd bounced out of range. MJ needed to get him down and make him stay down. At least temporarily. Another well-aimed punch landed on his jaw. The look of surprise, the shock, on his face would have been amusing at another time, but today she was too furious to think about the irony of this situation for long.

As he lunged to catch her, she kicked him in the groin. He yelled and bent, his hands moving to protect his private area. MJ was in no mood to spare him. She heard a loud noise, and then Dylan streaked through the main door. As he leapt over the couch, she pivoted and delivered a powerful jab to Rod's face with her elbow. It was enough to make him topple over and fall on the soft rug.

Blind with rage, she pounced on him but Dylan grabbed her wrist. "Easy, tiger." He enveloped her in a tight hug. "It's all right. You're all right. You got him, baby. You got him." His hands raced up and down her back. He lifted her face and saw the cut on her lips. "I'll get the ice."

"Call the police first," she said, panting.

Keeping his hand on her arm, he pulled her towards the phone, dialed 911, and made the call. Afterwards, he lifted her, put her on the high stool and dug out a bag of frozen peas from her refrigerator. She took it from his hand and held it against the cut.

Dylan spared a glance at Rod who was moaning as he made an effort to stand. "Who's he?"

"My ex-husband, Rod." Her voice was muffled as she spoke against the bag of peas.

Dylan strode over to Rod, grabbed his arm, and made him stand. "All right there, big guy?"

Rod nodded. "The bitch hit me."

MJ saw the flash of anger cross Dylan's

face. He raised his arm, pulled it back, and plowed his fist straight into Rod's face. The satisfying sound of crunch followed by Rod's scream as he toppled over once more warmed her heart.

"Oops!" Dylan said.

MJ suppressed a chuckle, the left side of her face hurt like crazy. "He's going to lawyer up and claim that we ganged up on him."

"Let him do his worst." Dylan walked up to MJ and removed the bag of peas. "The cut has stopped bleeding, but your lip is swollen. And that bruise on your cheek is going to turn a nasty shade of black and blue tomorrow." Gingerly, he ran a hand over it. "I'm sorry I broke your door."

She shook her head, hopped off the stool, and buried herself in his arms. She'd been an idiot for far too long. It was time to make amends and to realize what was really important in her life. How could she have been so stupid? She had a man who was devoted to her, loved her, and she was bent on wasting time on nonsensical issues.

"I could find it in my heart to forgive you for breaking my door but only if you forgive me for being an idiot, for doubting your love, and for being a complete ass."

As she gazed into his cool blue-green

eyes, her heart soared with joy. She knew she must look a sorry sight with her swollen eyes and bruised lips, but she didn't even care. All she cared about right now was that she was safe, safe in Dylan's arms.

Slowly, he brushed his lips over her cheek, kissing the bruise. "I suppose I could manage to do that, but it would take me an awfully long time to forgive you." He kissed her again. "It might even take me a lifetime, and you would have to stay with me until I was sure my heart was clear of any ill will."

She slipped her arms around his neck. "Well, I suppose, I could make an effort to suffer in order to appease you. A lifetime, you said?"

"Nothing less would do."

She sighed with pleasure and rested her head on his shoulder very delicately, mindful of her bruises. "I'm all yours then."

Suddenly, things were looking up.

Epilogue

MJ lifted her hand to admire the diamond ring that gleamed on her finger. "It's beautiful, isn't it?"

"Stop showing off. You're a lucky girl. Don't rub it in." Trudy finished her wine and poured herself another. They were celebrating MJ's engagement. Dylan had taken Sadie for a movie, and it was just the two of them in her apartment.

MJ laughed as she picked up her own glass. Indeed, she was lucky. Rod had made a lot of noise, tried to make it seem as if she'd called him over and assaulted him. But the police had done their job. Once they tracked his activities, it wasn't difficult to pin down the fact that he'd been in New York for much longer than he wanted them to believe. Not only had he stalked MJ, he'd slashed the tires on Dylan's car, left the dead rat on her doorstep, and vandalized her front door.

And for what? All in the hope of driving her scared and senseless into his manly arms.

MJ shook her head. Too bad that Rod had easily gotten bail. But the restraining order her lawyer had taken against him was enough to assure her that he would slink back to Boston and never disturb her again. It had been hard explaining all this to Sadie, but she'd managed to brush over some of the facts. Thank God, that day Sadie had been away at a friend's house. She had not witnessed her father's violence and her mother's resulting aggression. Would Rod have hit his own child? It was hard to say—and she was just glad it was all over.

"So Leslie and I get to be bridesmaids?" Trudy's question pulled MJ out of her reverie. "Please promise me that you would not make me wear an ugly dress."

She grinned. "I was thinking bright orange or perhaps neon green."

Trudy shuddered. "You're killing me."

She and Dylan hadn't yet decided where they would hold the ceremony or the date.

MJ wanted something stylish but simple in New York City. Dylan wanted a lavish, exotic destination wedding on a Caribbean island, either Tobago or Antigua. It would take some time to compromise and find the ideal venue. After all, no marriage was complete without a little give and take. And she looked forward to ironing out these differences with Dylan.

"I've got to be off now." Trudy said.

"Stay for dinner."

"Some other time, friend." Trudy hopped off the stool, swayed on her feet, and grabbed the counter for support. "Whoa! Some wine!"

"Dylan bought it. Stay a while. He'll be in soon, and he can drop you home."

"I'll call a cab." Trudy picked up her purse. She dug out her phone and placed the call.

Fifteen minutes later, MJ walked Trudy down, bundled her into the cab, and went back up. She stared at the door and shuddered at the memory of what Sadie had discovered there a few weeks ago. The writing on the walls and door was gone; after the police were done with it, Dylan had sand-papered and then painted it over, taking care to erase each and every horrible line and word.

She cleaned the counter, swept up the

evidence of Trudy and her celebration for two, and settled in on the couch. A few minutes later, the door opened and Dylan walked in with Sadie.

"You missed it, Mom. It was super," her daughter whopped with joy.

"Walking dead. Blood and gore. Spare me." She shuddered and scooted over as Dylan went over and sat by her side. He put his arms around her and kissed her.

"Ugh! I am going to my room." Sadie escaped.

"That girl!" MJ shook her head. "She can watch the dead bite other people and turn them into zombies, but she can't watch her own mother kiss her guy."

"Fiancé," Dylan reminded her, tapping his finger on her ring. "And soon-to-be husband."

MJ ran a hand over his cheek. "Mmm...I like the sound of that." As usual, she found it hard to believe that they were a couple. Her concerns about their age difference were a thing of the past. What had she done to deserve such a man? He was awesome. The way he interacted with her daughter, the ease with which he slipped into her routine, and the way he cherished her as if she were a goddess made her wonder if she was dreaming.

But of course, the man kissing her

cheeks, her jaw, and the skin of her throat wasn't a figment of her imagination. He was real—and he was all hers.

Finally, she'd found her bliss. MJ sighed with pleasure as she leaned back, her arms twisting around his neck as she pulled him closer.

Life couldn't get any better.

THE END

About the Author

Thank you for taking a chance on *TRAINING HER CURVES* and trusting me to give you a few hours of reading pleasure. I'd be happy if you do me a favor. Many potential readers depend on honest reviews to determine if they should 1-Click a book. Please help them make an informed decision by posting a review of *TRAINING HER CURVES*. Your review doesn't have to be long.

I love hearing from readers, so you may shoot me an email to author.roxywilson@gmail.com. That's how our friendship will begin, if we aren't friends already.

I also hope you'll consider joining my mailing list. By doing this, you'll receive updates on my upcoming releases, giveaways, deals and free reads. It will surely be an honor if you decide to subscribe. To join my mailing list, visit https://dl.bookfunnel.com/zv2wi4w57y.

Kind regards, always!
Roxy

Books by Roxy Wilson
Second Chance Romance:
Alessandro Mancini
Friends to Forever
Meant to Be

Holiday Romance:
Be With You: A Valentine's Romance
A Holly Jolly Christmas (Merry Matrimony, Book 1)
The Gift of Maggie (Merry Matrimony, Book 2)
Wynter Wonderland (Merry Matrimony, Book 3)
Loving St. Nick

Secret Baby/Pregnancy Romance:
A Lesson in Love
The Law of Love
Baby Wanted (A Bundle of Joy, Book 1)

The Baby Proposal (A Bundle of Joy, Book 2)
Baby, You're Mine (A Bundle of Joy, Book 3)
Secret Baby Seduction (A Bundle of Joy, Book 4)
This Time, Baby (A Bundle of Joy, Book 5)

Shapeshifter/Paranormal Romance:
Greer's Alphas
My Guardian Vampire
Bree's Purr-fect Mate
Nya's Wolf: BBW Paranormal Shape Shifter Romance
Fur-ever Yours: A BBW Paranormal Shape Shifter Romance (The Protectors Volume 1)
Fur-ever Yours: A BBW Paranormal Shape Shifter Romance (Volumes 1 & 2)
Fur-Ever Yours: A BBW Paranormal Shape Shifter Romance (The Protectors Book 2)
My Guardian Vampire, Volume 1

Cowboy/Western Romance:
Just Gettin' Started: BWWM Interracial Cowboy/Western Romance (Westbury Ranch, Book 1)
Stay With Me: BWWM Interracial Cowboy/Western Romance (Westbury Ranch Book 2)

I Only Have Eyes For You: BWWM Cowboy/Western Romance (Westbury Ranch Book 3)

Other Books:
BRUISED (An MMA Fighter Romance)
Take This Ring

Boxed Sets:
Baby Love Volume 1
Baby Love Volume 2
Yuletide Love Volume 1
Yuletide Love Volume 2

Made in the USA
Coppell, TX
04 July 2021